Courage to Leave!

COURAGE TO LEAVE!

Acquanetta Kommenus

Copyright © 2008 by Acquanetta Kommenus.

The book cover photo and author photo belongs solely to the author:
Acquanetta Kommenus

ISBN:	Hardcover	978-1-4363-5706-7
	Softcover	978-1-4363-5705-0

All rights reserved. No part of this book may be reproduced or transmitted in any form or by any means, electronic or mechanical, including photocopying, recording, or by any information storage and retrieval system, without permission in writing from the copyright owner.

This is a work of fiction. Names, characters, places and incidents either are the product of the author's imagination or are used fictitiously, and any resemblance to any actual persons, living or dead, events, or locales is entirely coincidental.

This book was printed in the United States of America.

To order additional copies of this book, contact:
Xlibris Corporation
1-888-795-4274
www.Xlibris.com
Orders@Xlibris.com
51908

Contents

1	—	Get out!	13
2	—	Too Little Time	15
3	—	First Hunting Trip	17
4	—	Beginning of School	20
5	—	The Razor Strap	25
6	—	First Field Trip	27
7	—	Playing	30
8	—	Band Practice	32
9	—	Why Me?	37
10	—	First Born	42
11	—	Baby Girl	49
12	—	Going Home!	60
13	—	Believe in Chain Letters?	64
14	—	The Thief That Got Away!	67
15	—	Telling all!	69
16	—	Where's the Beef?	75
17	—	Strange Nights	80
18	—	Christian	83
19	—	Horses!	94
20	—	U.F.O.?	98
21	—	The Last Beating	101
22	—	Dedicated to My Sister and Mother	111
23	—	Final Years	118
24	—	Courage to Leave	129

25 —	Last Time	137
26 —	Liar, Liar	143
27 —	After Liar, Liar	146
28 —	Dedicated to My Guardian Angel	149
29 —	Snakes!	158
30 —	Struggling . . .	165
31 —	Conclusion	169
32 —	The Author	173

Date: Wed, 04 Jan 2006 22:18:54-0700

New Subject: COURAGE TO LEAVE!

Dear Marion,

I have read all of your stories. Thank you for sharing so much with me! After reading them, I sat and thought for a long while, and I wrote down a list of words that describe the abuse that you have been subjected to throughout your life. I want to share them with you:

Beating	Control
Humiliation	Callousness
Pain	Deprivation
Shame	Fear
Mental cruelty	Terror
Child abuse	Loneliness
Ridicule	Panic
Brutality	Hopelessness
Hate	Abandonment
Starvation	Forced marriage
Spitefulness	Torture
Vengeance	Horror
Anger	Sadism
Isolation	Rejection
Sexual abuse	

Most people only encounter a few of these things, and then only the least severe of those on the list. But you Marion, have been battered, traumatized, and assaulted relentlessly by all of these things, and more! Most women would not be able to endure a fraction of what you have been through. And yet, you have survived! You are still alive to tell about all of these horrible experiences. You fought back and endured!! And I know that you bear many scars, both physical and emotional. But still you have SURVIVED!! I salute you for your strength, courage, and endurance in the face of insurmountable hardships! You have my total respect!

In no way do I think any less of you after reading all of this. In fact, I hold you in higher esteem now than before. I don't think you are crazy, and I don't see you as a different person now than before. I see you as a more complete person now that I know so many of the personal details of your life.

If I had been in your shoes, I don't believe I would have survived. To me, you are the ULTIMATE SURVIVOR Marion Heliconia!

Ms. Kommenus this is how the stories you wrote made me feel about the character Marion. It took a lot of work I know to write them with such strong feelings.

I continue to pray for you every day!

Your eternal friend,
Johnny

Date: 06 Jan 2006

Hi Marion,

That is a wonderful testimony to your strength and courage through the years when you have suffered so much. I agree with everything Johnny has said. I can only admire you for the way you have coped with so much evil in your life and come through it all. These are my feeling for you, the leading character in these stories.

Hugs,
Caroline

Acknowledgements

By Acquanetta Kommenus

Friends from around the world: California, England, Colorado, Alaska, and Sweden, have spent many hours listening to me cry over the past year. For this I am eternally grateful, for their understanding, patience, encouragement, and motivation. It seemed that not just one or two, but even more, would show up as a friend in my greatest hour of need. From the bottom of my heart, I thank all of you for your help. It has been extremely hard for the last few years to write the stories about Marion.

Starting with my dear friend, Johnny, you spent many hours motivating me. You made me see that I did have the strength to complete my book. Without your guidance, I could never have finished the stories. You went even further with your faith in my work, and spent many hours reading and editing the stories. For that I will forever owe you, Johnny, a gracious gratitude for life. Thank you, my special friend, for all of your time and faith in me, and for making me see that Marion had the: COURAGE TO LEAVE!

Thanks to my English girlfriend, Caroline; you have spent many hours with me on the phone, lending your shoulder for me to cry on. Many times you have built my confidence and encouraged me to continue my work. Thank you Caroline, you're a great friend to have.

My Alaskan friend, Shady, you have listened to me with understanding, and let me know that I can help people to enjoy the best of each day while I wrote about Marion. So many times I thought I was losing control as I put myself in her place, and you helped me to make it through some of my most difficult times. You have spent many hours with me playing Internet pool, to get me to relax so I could continue working. Thank you Shady!

To each and every one of you, you'll always be in my heart for participating in my time of need and writing your feelings for Marion.

My Love to you All!

Acquanetta Kommenus

Get Out!

People can talk and point their fingers all they want at women who are abused. Some women, like Marion, have been raised to believe that this is the way of life. We don't know any better, because we never lived any other way! Marion thought when she left her mother's home to have her own, that it would be different. But it wasn't; the abuse only got worse for her. She had heard of other women who called the police for help. The wife would sign for a warrant, thinking, "Now he'll stop hitting me." Then she would see him walk in the door the next morning with his fists doubled up to teach her a lesson. Some husbands pet, pamper, and treat their wives like princesses to get them to drop the charges, then mess them up so bad that they are too ashamed for anyone to see them. But they all know not to call the police, because it only makes matters worse. Marion learned what not to do by listening to other women.

Later, she heard of another law that came out: if you called for help, they arrested both husband and wife. She still can't help thinking, why do they think that is a better solution? At the age of 47, Marion was still too frightened to call the police. She stayed hidden in the house for weeks with her battered face, ashamed to ask for help, or afraid to try to run away.

Several years after the last beating, a neighbor had heard about it (how, she didn't know), but she lived right across the street from her. She said that Marion's family were very peaceful, hard—working people, who never bothered anyone, and were very quiet. When she asked Marion about the bruises, She felt like it was time to start telling the truth, but only a very small part to stop the lady's curiosity. Marion said, "You'd be surprised what goes on behind closed doors." Then she told her story. The neighbor had never suspected anything.

Later Marion stood on the porch looking down her street. Only, 150 yards from Marion's house, other husband's fists were also abusing their wives. One lady's husband beat her just for the hell of it when he was drunk. The one right across the street from her wouldn't even step out of her yard for fear of a beating; she was going blind from so many hits to her head. Marion had met all of the women on her street. Outside of one or two, every woman on her street was being abused. How could she help them? She didn't know where to start for help; so she ran as hard as she could to save her own life.

Even today, Marion still feels as if she's being punished for something. She knew from the past she'd rather be abused physically than mentally. Physically, it's over until the next time; mentally, it's never over! But what did she do to deserve being slapped, beaten, raped, punished, threatened, and poisoned? After reading her stories, please tell her; do you know why?

Marion begs and plead with any woman who is being abused, "Get out! Don't choose physical or mental abuse; we should never have to make a decision like this. Make the decision to live life. Today there is help, she promises you! Yes! Marion knows how hard it is to start over, but the existing abusive life is not the way. Young or old, none of us deserves to be abused! Never feel like it's too late! For God's sake, GET OUT!!!! There are people in your area that will help you! Please, if you know someone or see anyone, woman or a child, help them, please!" But remember, anyone that cries wolf, beware, one day the wolf will come, but help won't be there! Now she tells some of her stories . . . .

Too Little Time

I remember my mother crying, but could never understand why. We went to Papa Jacks house and there were several people there that I recognized. By the front windows there was a bed in the room. In the opposite corner was a gas heater. So I know the weather had to be cold, because several women were backed up to the heater. I went to the bed, and it was Papa Jack lying there. He put his hand on my shoulder, and I laid my head on his side. He told them to get my box to stand on. Someone in the room told me to get away from him. I distinctly remember him saying: "Leave her alone! Marion's not hurting anything!" That's where I stayed napping off and on; looking at my Papa Jack, not knowing this would be my only memory of him.

Looking back now, I can remember the love I felt from him. Maybe that explains as the two men in white were going out the door with my Papa Jack, I ran to them grabbing him, screaming at the top of my lungs, "NO, NO, YOU CAN'T TAKE MY PAPA JACK!" My mother tried to pull me away, but I was holding on to my Papa so tight that she asked for help. It took Aunt Rosie, Aunt Gwen, Mother and her stepmother, Beth, to hold me. As I was screaming "THEY TOOK MY PAPA; I WANT HIM BACK! PLEASE BRING MY PAPA BACK! MOTHER PLEASE MAKE

THEM BRING MY PAPA JACK BACK, I'LL BE A GOOD GIRL I PROMISE!!!!" I heard some of the women making rude remarks about me. I didn't care; I just wanted my papa back! Today I know the date; it was December the 12th, 1950. At the age of four years and four months, I didn't know that he would be the last person who would ever love me.

A few days later I remember my mother and daddy sitting in the front seat of the car on the side of a road. I was standing on the hump in the back floor of the car listening. Mother was crying, and I looked past her direction. There was a small crowd of people. I recognized some of them and my Aunts. "Mother, can we go and see what they are doing?" I asked. "No!" she screamed. "Marion, you fixed that where I can't go down there!" She never explained what was going on. I never understood what she meant until I wrote this. Maybe this is why my mother hated me for the rest of her life.

When I reached adulthood, I realized that day so long ago was a funeral, but I couldn't remember where it was. My mother died at the age of 58, and she was buried in the same grave yard as my Papa Jack in December 1978. At the age of thirty-two I finally found where they had put my dearly beloved Papa Jack. On one side of that graveyard laid the last person who loved me so many years ago. On the other side laid the person who hated me for so many years. Yet, I loved them both dearly.

First Hunting Trip

Fall 1951

I was outside and could hear my mother and daddy arguing. They did that a lot after the twins, Lacy and Lynn arrived. Before they were born, my daddy would take me everywhere he went: to the store, to the neighbors, and to town. Afterwards, he never even spoke to me unless it was necessary. That morning I heard my mother say, "Take Marion with you; what's it going to hurt?" He told my mother he was going hunting and I would make too much noise. We lived half-way down Cool Springs Mountain, where he was going to hunt squirrels. Needless to say, he lost the argument. Mother was ten years older than he was.

After he jerked me by the hand, I started to cry. He had never hurt me like that before. Then he cussed, and told me to shut up, or he and Mother would argue again. I got very quiet. Up on the mountain we went, with me right behind my daddy, feeling so proud. Then he turned, making a mean face at me, "Shhhhhhh!" He didn't understand the leaves I stepped on were making the noise. How could I be quiet? After walking a long ways, he said, "Come here, Marion." I thought he was going to carry me, but instead he sat me up on a tall, huge stump. He whispered, "you be quiet". He told me he wouldn't be far away, and said nothing would bother me as long as I was quiet. I cried, "Daddy, please don't leave me, please!" His voice changed, sounding like a growl, saying "Shut up now, or I'll leave you on that stump for good and let the wild animals take you away!"

With my pleas turning into sobs, I tried to be quiet. I didn't want him to leave me. It was so high that I couldn't jump. The last I saw of him was his back as he disappeared into the woods. I sat very quietly, listening. I could hear him going farther away from me until I could hear nothing at all. With my little heart pounding so hard, I heard something in the leaves. "Oh, no; it's coming closer. I've got to pee-pee. Where is my daddy?" I whispered, "Dadddddyyyyy, where are you? Dadddddyyyyy, I've got to pee-pee!" I rocked back and forth holding myself, whispering over and over: "Daddy, I'm scared!" All of a sudden, the noise got so close that I screamed and peed at the same time!

After I screamed four or five times, he showed up laughing at me. Then he saw that my clothes were wet and made more fun of me. From that day forward for the rest of my life, he made fun of everything about me. As I grew up, it was "Bozo feet, Dumbo ears, ski-jump nose, sandpaper skin, knock knees and cow factory!" You see, I always loved him as my father, because I didn't know anything different. I could never figure out why he hated me so much after Lacy and Lynn were born, making me feel as if I had done something wrong every day. I spent many years of my life trying to make it right, only to find out he WASN'T MY FATHER!! He never told me again that he loved me. I went to see him more than a year ago hoping he had missed me since he had not seen me in many years. He just looked at me and sniggered as he sat down for five minutes staring at me. I was polite, asking how he was, hoping he would say something to stop the pain that tortured me all of my life as why he hated me. He rose, turned his back on me, disappearing into the house. A few months later, his second wife, Marsha, died; two weeks later, he died. It may be cold of me, but not a tear fell for him, and I felt no grief what-so-ever for him. He never said why he hated me.

Beginning of School, 1952

The first day of school was an exciting day for me. As Mother brushed my blonde curls, she told me what all I had to say and do, of course, alone. Holding my few school belongings, my heart began to pound very hard. "Please go with me, Mother. I'm scared!" I begged. "Go to Harris's store, and the bus will come for you. Now go Marion!" Mother demanded as she pushed me out the door, closing it behind me. I walked down the hill three blocks alone to the bus stop.

When the bus arrived all the seats had been taken. The bus driver told me to move to the back; then he left for the next stop. My body was pushed against the back door of the bus as I was holding onto the handles of the last two seats. The bus took a turn going up a hill. I screamed at the top of my lungs, trying to grab the girl in front of me. Out the back door we both went. I landed on top of her, breaking her arm, but the bus didn't stop. It was rolling back over us. I pulled the girl to the middle so the bus tires wouldn't roll over her. An ambulance came for the girl, and a man in a car took me to school, not back home.

At school, they put me in an empty classroom alone and told me to stay there. Then a woman and a man came in. Scared of what they would do to me, I hid under a desk. I was crying, shaking, and afraid to move. The man said, "I believe she's ok, just frightened, but if anything occurs, don't hesitate to call me." Even more was to happen when I got home and told Mother about my day. It scared me when she began screaming over the event. On my report card the teacher had written that Marion was a very sweet little girl, but she seems to be withdrawn.

The second year they had divided the busloads, so I had to wait for the second bus. That meant standing in front of the school to wait. There was a boy, Kyle who liked me. He would pull my hair or run by, saying, "Tag, you're it!" This particular day Kyle yanked my hair hard, and I ran after him to get him to stop. New gravel on the drive way caused me to slide down. Being the tough little girl I was, I just jumped up and ran again. I couldn't catch him, so I went back to wait for the bus.

Some of the other girls that were waiting told me that there was blood all over the back of my head. "No, there's not!" I replied, feeling no pain. "Go to the office now Marion, you're bleeding, bad!" they said. I put my hand to the back of my head, discovering that it was wet. As I looked at my hand, it was covered with blood. A sick feeling hit the pit of my stomach, I went to the office without saying a word. My worst fear was to think of what my mother would say or do.

Were the teachers scared or what? They placed me in a car with the windows up and said for me not to move. I can still feel the sweat running from my brow; it was so hot. I don't know how long I sat there, but they finally took me home. My mother took a wet cloth, trying to clean the wound on my head. She fussed and cussed about the dry blood matted in my long hair. The hole was the size of a silver dollar. She cut long strands of my hair where the blood had dried from the heat. Later I heard Mother telling a neighbor that I had stayed in the car for three-and-a-half hours on that hot summer day. Report card time my teacher wrote again: "Marion is a sweet child, but she seems to be withdrawn. Is there a problem at home?" "Please call if I can help."

Third grade came and went. Even today I still visualize those days with wonder. I was over fifty when I last looked at my report cards from the past and remember the fourth grade all too well. There was never any breakfast for me. When lunchtime came, I had to sit and watch my classmates eat a hot lunch. As I watched them dispose of their remaining lunches, my stomach rumbled from hunger. I stared in the trashcan at all of the food, wondering if I could grab a handful and hide to eat it, but I kept quiet.

One of my classmates, Annie, who lived a short distance from school invited me to lunch. I saw no reason not to go, so we walked and laughed to her house. I didn't realize how much I was eating until I saw her mother watching me, then she asked, "Marion, when was the last time you had anything to eat?" "Yesterday," I answered. It was time for us to walk back. It was the first time that year that I wasn't hungry in school. This would be another day I would remember for the rest of my life! As the two of us entered class the teacher, Mrs. Sheldon was waiting. She told Annie to go sit at her desk. Then all hell broke out for me. "Marion, into the cloakroom!" The teacher had her four-inch by two foot board with holes in her hand. She asked why I left the school grounds. I explained that I was hungry and was invited to go. Mrs. Sheldon told me to lean over, with my hands against the wall. I screamed as the board pounded on my backside ten times. Then Mrs. Sheldon said, "I will call your MOTHER!!!!" I begged "Oh please! Don't call her! PLEASE!" She continued, "If she doesn't whip you Marion, I'll do it again tomorrow!" All of the pain I could feel disappeared when the fear of Mother's fury entered my body. I cried the rest of the day, as classmates laughed with their sly remarks to me. "Oh, you're going to get it now Marion!" I walked home very slowly, knowing what was to come. I saw the long hickory stick, and knew Mother had been to the woods and waiting for me.

The next day, with my eyes swollen and bloody stripes on my legs, I arrived in the classroom in a daze. Mrs. Sheldon stared in disbelief; she took me into the cloakroom, and questioned me. "Marion who did this to you? Did your mother?" I stood with tears rolling down my cheeks, not of pain, but of shame, and nodded yes. We walked to the principal's office. She sat in a chair and said, "Marion, I am so sorry. I'll never call your mother again! Never!" Then she hugged me. I learned that no matter how hungry I was, it was better to starve than to take a beating. I never left the school grounds again. On my report card was written: "Marion is a wonderful child, very smart, but she seems to be withdrawn. Is there a problem at home? Does your family need help?"

That year my family moved back and forth to West Virginia about six times. When we moved back home I had to go back to the third grade, even though I had passed to the fourth grade before we left. I had several bad experiences while attending school up north. It was the first time in my life that I can remember a man molesting me. There was nothing left to do but to repeat the fourth grade when we returned home.

Things seemed to be okay for me except for my secrets until the sixth grade. One of my classmates, Stacy had brought her lunch to school, but had told me she was going home for lunch. Before lunch I went into the cloakroom and unwrapped her banana sandwich; it smelled so good. When lunchtime came I took the lunch outside, hid, and ate it, pretending my mother had made them for me, I was so hungry. When I went back to class, the teacher, Mrs. Lange was waiting and began to ask me what I had for lunch. Well, of course, a banana sandwich. She said Stacy's lunch had disappeared, and that I had to be the one who took it. With my stomach full, I knew what my mother would do to me if she found out. The only thing I knew to do was to lie. I knew it was wrong and I never did it again.

Later that year I met a redheaded girl, her name was Kathy. She said that I could sit with her in the lunchroom. I would watch her eat and later ask if she had finished eating, knowing she could hear my stomach rumbling from hunger. Sometimes Kathy would tell me to go ahead and eat it, but other times she would jerk the tray up and toss it into the trash. A couple of months later, Mrs. Lange called me to walk with her to the office. Several teachers and the principal were in the room as we entered. Fear swelling up in my chest and throat made tears swell in my eyes, they told me not to cry. They were just trying to figure out a way to help me. No one had ever helped me, so why now? Later I found out that Kathy's mother had called the school about me begging for food from her daughter. I didn't beg, I waited until she was finished. The teachers asked several questions, such as "Marion, what did you have to eat before coming to school?" and "Why is it you never bring a lunch to school?" I thought before I answered. Then I asked, "Are you going to call my mother?" They said, "No." They had seen my legs striped with the bloody whelps more than once, and they knew what would happen if they called her. I dropped my head and said I never had anything to eat until suppertime, but I had to wait until everyone else ate first. Then I could eat what was left, if anything, and the scraps from the others' plates as I washed the dishes. I didn't see anything wrong with it. After that I had to work in the lunchroom to pay for my lunches. For the rest of the year I never went hungry again in school. But my mother gave me even less to eat at night after she found out about it, and sometimes gave me nothing. She would make me stay outside until they had finished, then call me in to do the dishes. Many times I licked all of the plates before washing them to keep from being so hungry at night.

No one knew about my stepfather's friend molesting me for three years during this time, and no one knew about the man up north who tried to insert himself into me when I was nine. I would beg mother to let me stay home, always the same, "Do as I say!" I hated going, every night he made me do the same thing after he sent his wife and children to bed.

The teacher wrote on my report card: "Marion is a sweet girl, but her withdrawal problems are worse and causing her grades to drop more. Can you give me a call or come to a consultation to see if we can help her?" I never told anyone what had happened to me, but I did pass to the seventh grade. What I didn't know was that my hunger pains would start over again, even more than before, but I kept quiet.

The Razor Strap

I never knew what a razor strap was until my mother explained it to me. It belonged to her papa because he shaved with a straightedge razor. He was born in 1886 and died in 1950. His entire life he used the same strap to sharpen his razor. By the time I was nine I had learned to hate that strap. My mother used it on me for everything when she was angry, or if I looked at her the wrong way. I wasn't allowed to look my mother in the eye. Anything people told her she believed, it didn't matter if they lied to her or not. One particular time I was about 10 and we lived on the second floor of an apartment building at 209 Gravel Street in Limon, West Virginia. Downstairs, lived a family of three: Mr. And Mrs. Hayes and their 16-year-old daughter, Gail. She became friends with me, but not for long.

You would have to know my mother to understand that I wasn't allowed to have friends. So Gail became my mother's friend. One day Gail said she would shop for mother, and I could go with her. We didn't have to go too far, but then she held my hand and would jerk me across the street. Then, on the sidewalk, I told her she didn't have to hold my hand. Gail insisted, and continued jerking me as if I were a dog on a leash resisting to walk forward. I started crying and asked her why she was hurting me. She said, "Your mother said I could." I finally got my hand from Gail. She said if I didn't hold her hand that I couldn't go. I said ok, that I would stand right there to wait for her. She went on, but there were so many people I couldn't see where she went. I stood there nearly four hours. It started getting dark, so I went home.

When I entered the door, there sit Gail with my mother. So much fear built up in my chest until I thought it would burst. Mother told her to go home, that she didn't need to see what I had coming. I told Mother the truth, but it didn't do any good. As always, she never believed me. I had to sit in the chair until she came back. When she walked in, I could feel the pain before she ever hit me the first time. She would hold my arm, hitting me with the razor strap on my back, butt, and legs. She loved to hit my legs, leaving large whelps with blood oozing out. I can't count the times I begged her not to hit me so hard. "Mother! Please, don't hit me! I didn't do anything wrong! Please stop!" Worst of all she would make me go outside and stand on the street where people could see my legs. I'll never forget her words: "This way people can see what a horrible bitch you are!" How could I be so bad? I had my little brother and four-year-old twin sisters to take care of. What did I do, for her to say I was so terrible?

Later way after dark Mother would call me inside. She told me to take my bath and go to bed. That night she talked to my stepfather, and they were laughing at what she did to me. He had to leave for work and Mother went to take her bath. I jumped up and ran to find the razor strap looking for a place to hide it. I knew of a secret place in the bottom of the closet, so I laid flat on the floor and pushed it as far back as I could. Jumping back into bed, I knew that would be the last time she would ever hit me with the RAZOR STRAP!

First Field Trip 1957

Many years ago after my stepfather was discharged from the military we were never able to travel again. So when it came to my class going on a field trip I knew it would be so much fun since I had never been to a Zoo. My teacher Mrs. Corbin called me aside and told me that I couldn't go unless I had something new to wear on the trip. Pain hit my heart since I still had to wear the clothes I had the year before. When I got home I told mother what she had said. Mother cussed and ranted as usual. Out the door I went to climb the tree to get on top of the house. I didn't want to hear that I couldn't go. I could still hear her, but I could lie there so if she decided to take it out on me, she wouldn't be able to find me. Later it got quiet, making sure no one could see me go down the tree since it was my spot, I slid down the tree to go into the house. Not saying anything in fear she would get angry again, I did as I was told. Without a doubt I knew not to make any mistakes, knowing all mother needed was one reason to swear at me that I couldn't go. As we were eating supper she and my step dad talked about me going on the field trip. Standing there (no place for me to sit) I ate very slowly while listening. They had no money for any new clothes. As I looked at Lacy and Lynn's clothes, then looked at mine. I had never thought about it before, they had on new clothes and I'm still wearing last year's school clothes. They don't even go to school yet! But I knew better than to say anything. The water was heating for me to wash the dishes so I started clearing the table. After, I heated more water to give the twins and our brother their bath. I did everything without being told what to do in hopes I would get to go to the Zoo. All week my fear would rise up that I wouldn't get to go even though I had already paid the five cents for the bus fare and mother said she still doesn't know. Later that night as I lay on the bed getting my three siblings to sleep I could hear the old singer sewing machine going. I closed my eyes hoping . . . . Mother woke me the next morning saying she had a surprise for me. I jumped up and there it was. She said for me to try it on, I did, it fit! I loved it! It's NEW!!!!!!!! I can go to the ZOO!!!! I wanted to hug mother, but I knew better. That she didn't allow, so I jumped up and down and around in circles. I brushed my hair and pranced off to the bus stop with a proud smile on my face. I should have known it was too good to last long. When I arrived at the bus stop, everyone was sniggering, pointing and whispering. I ask them did they like my new dress? They laughed hysterically then. On the verge of tears I ask them why were they laughing at me? The girl Joanie, sitting next to me told them to shut up! I felt frightened, wondering why were they laughing at me? As I walked into the classroom my teacher's mouth dropped open as she stared at me. I ask her if she like my new dress? She commented, well at least it's new. My heart broke and the tears ran down my face as I looked at my classmate sniggering, whispering and pointing at me. When I looked at their clothes, not one single person had on new clothes and as I sit at my desk the teacher said, that's enough! So we lined up in a row to go to the bus. I didn't know why I was the only one with new clothes on, why were they making fun of me? Once on the way my classmate, Nellie, that sit next to me told everyone to shush, that I couldn't help what my parents did. What did they do? Why doesn't anyone have on new clothes? Why did everyone make fun of me, I just couldn't understand. This is supposed to be a fun day for me and I am crying feeling like an outcast. Nellie sit next to me said not to worry, they are just jealous as we arrived at the Zoo. She made me feel better and we looked at the animals and listened to the teacher explain about each one of them. That's what I want to do when I grow up, just take care of all the animals I can with lots of love. We walked out to where tables were to have our lunch. After the teacher told us to wash our hands so the animals couldn't smell food on us. When my turn came to wash my hands the boys were coming by drying their hands on my new dress. Telling them to stop it, they laughed even harder. Shaking my head I asked them why did they do it? Laughing they said, you dumb idiot, don't you know you're wearing two towels sewed together???? The sobs came and I ran as hard as I could to get away from everybody. That's why they were making fun of me! I knew it was towels, but it was my NEW DRESS!!! All the way home I didn't say a word, just stared out the window so I wouldn't have to see anyone else laugh at me. Mother took one look at me and asked what is wrong? I cried like a baby and told her the story of my supposing wonderful day at the Zoo. Didn't bother her, she said, go change before you mess up my new towels, I did, and then watched as she pulled the threads from the seams. My new dress that I was so proud of that morning was now turned into folded towels. Back up the tree I went to lie on the roof to cry in silence for my horrible first visit to the Zoo.

Playing 1960

One day my stepfather was playing with his twins, Lacy and Lynn. I just stood on the side and watched. I could see he was getting the best of them. Lynn started crying, but Lacy was determined not to let him make her cry. Her anger got the best of her and she hurt him as he had hurt her. I just watched calling mother, she called out for me to stay out of it. He said a few cuss words as he started for Lacy. I started yelling for her to run as he was taking off his belt. I knew she was in for it. She ran out the driveway down to the street and around the corner. Before she could make it to the front gate he caught her. I screamed for Mother and she said, "Leave them alone Marion; they're his kids and he can do what he wants with them." He whipped Lacy very hard, leaving her in the ditch crying, then he came back to the house with his belt in his hand.

I just stood at the corner of the house staring at him. Tears running down my face, not knowing how to help my little sisters, I had always taken care of them. If looks could kill, he would have dropped dead right then. He looked up at me and asked, "Don't you like it?" I told him he was playing too rough with them, but when they hurt him back, he took advantage of the situation and whipped Lacy for the same thing he was doing to her. I told him they were little and he was a man; it wasn't fair to them. He told me to shut up or else he would let me have some of the same thing. When he turned around, I was still staring hard at him. He said, "What the hell, you're not my daughter!" He took the end of the belt with the holes and wrapped it around his hand, drawing back to swing the belt, he wrapped the buckle around my leg, and the prong went into my knee. With blood spurting out, my anger flew out of control. Screaming at him, "You will never hit my sisters or me again!" As he swung the belt I ran, shoving him backwards. He stood up screaming, cussing, and swinging the belt at me again. I got my chance to run into the house, hoping Mother would stop him. I screamed, "Mother! Please make him stop!" As always, she sat at the kitchen table with her coffee, cigarettes, and newspaper. Not even glancing up, she said, "Oh, you two stop it." As I entered the hallway, he grabbed my hair and slammed me into the wall, landing on my back on the floor. He picked me up by the yoke of my shirt, cussing and punching me in the face with his fist. Each time he hit me, I blacked out. When I hit the floor it woke me. Gritting my teeth, I'd run at him again. Next to the last time, I couldn't get up and kicked him as hard as I could in his crotch, hoping it would keep him off of me until I could get out of the house. I just had time to get up when he pounced on top of me, punching me over and over with his fist. There was no way I could get him off of me.

As I opened my eyes to see where the screams were coming from, I could see Lacy crying and screaming to the top of her lungs, "Mother! Mother! Daddy's killing Marion! Help her, please!" He had picked me up by the yoke of my shirt again, drawing back, giving me one more hard punch that knocked me into the next room. It took all of my strength to get up. As I got to the door, a hand touched me on the chest, it was Mother. She said, "Marion, you've had enough." I fell to the floor. I heard her tell my step-dad, "Damn Carl, I thought you were playing with her; I didn't know you were fighting." He replied, "Next time I'll kill her! I don't know why you wanted to keep her anyway! She's just another mouth to feed!"

Band Practice

The summer had been a long, hot, lonesome one, just staying on my parents' property, not going anywhere or doing anything, except work for them. There were the twins and my little brother Gary, for me to take care of. With the house cleaning and laundry, there was never any time or place for myself. Sometimes I'd climb a tree at the back of the house to gaze at the stars from the roof, so I looked forward to going back to school. Entering my first year in junior high was exciting, and a little frightening at the same time. On my first day I went to school barefooted. That's what I did the year before at grammar school. I wondered why the other kids had their shoes on. Not five minutes in the classroom, the teacher sent me to the office. The assistant principal, Mr. Waverly asked me where my shoes were. I told him they were in a drainpipe close to home, so they wouldn't get dirty. They must last all year, sometimes two. That day I learned my lesson well; I must wear shoes in Junior High. What I didn't know was that it would rain that very afternoon. My new oxfords were full of red mud when I got off of the bus. The only thing I remember from that day is that I had to clean them without mother finding out.

One of my favorite classes turned out to be physical education, with all of the girls exercising, making our selves sweat. Then after, we would go to the girls' locker room. The teacher told us we needed gym suits as soon as possible. How would I ask my mother without being in trouble? Asking for something was virtually impossible; my heart began to beat faster. Then we were told to hit the showers, brave girl was I, unbuttoning my blouse, until I saw the other girls strip, baring their beautiful white underwear. "Oh no! I can't do this!" My heart was racing! "What am I going to do?" You see, my underwear was very dingy, as grey as dirt: clean, but old. There were only two bras and panties for me to wear every day until they would fall apart, and these were nearly two years old. No, no, no! I couldn't pull my clothes off in front of the girls. I managed to stay in gym for a couple of weeks. After hearing my classmates make fun of another girl's underwear that looked like mine, I had to get out! The teacher noticed that I stayed by myself; later she told me to go to her office. We talked or rather she talked, warning me that if I didn't get my gym suit, she would fail me. I said nothing, just cried. When I got home that day, Mother was waiting for me. The teacher had called her, not knowing my fear of Mother. I didn't want to go home, I knew what was coming. Mother screamed until I told her everything. No more P.E. for me.

Somehow I managed to get in band; no money had to be spent. The school provided me with a French horn and later, a uniform. For the first time in my life, I felt as if I belonged to something. C-band and B-band, then A-band at the age of 15. We practiced long hours marching in the field with our instruments. The band director, Mr. Claymore, was a short, little round man with a great sense of humor. He was a person that I wished to be around more often, and he didn't punish me when I made a mistake. He was just a nice, understanding person helping me to better myself. He went beyond the call of duty for many of us.

There was no way Mr. Claymore could have known what would happen after practice on a hot summer day about a month after school began in August. It was the one-day that I felt so good when I did all the right things on the field with my marching and playing. Mr. Claymore praised me, I knew my face had a huge smile, I felt so proud. It was after school hours, so the buses were gone. As many other times, Mr. Claymore would overload his little car with as many of us as he could pack in it. Then he would proceed to see us safely home. On this particular day, he asked a senior, Mike, to take me home, since I only lived a mile from him. Of course, no problem, he would be glad to. I felt so proud with such an achievement at practice, and now to have a ride with the famous senior, but in the back of my mind I knew mother would make me pay dearly for being in his car. I could already see her hickory with thorns coming at me. For now I wanted to enjoy my ride home. We left first in Mike's blue-and white car, a very nice one. He opened the door for me, and off we went. I knew that I'd be home in ten minutes. When the first turn came up, he passed it. FEAR! PANIC! WARNING! My voice shaking, I asked, "Mike, why didn't you turn?" Smiling, he turned to me, saying he wanted to show me a house that his mom thought about buying. "It's not too far up here," he said. I had never been in that area; then he turned the car around. "Mike where's the house?" I asked. He pulled over and cut the motor off. I asked, "What are you doing?" Scared, I told him he didn't know my mother! "I have to go home!" He leaned over to kiss me. With my back against the door, I tried to get away from him. Then he backed up and said, "Ok Marion, I'll take you home." I was shaking, crying, and scared to death, with my heart going so fast. "Oh, God, Mother will kill me if she ever hears of this!" Believing him, I turned to sit facing the front. "Please take me home Mike, please!" I pleaded. He smiled, and then all of a sudden someone came from the back, grabbing me under my arms. It was Jake, he said, "Not until we get what we want; you think this is a free ride?" One of them was holding me, and the other one was trying to get my panties off! I was screaming, begging, pleading, "PLEASE, PLEASE DON'T DO THIS! PLEASE, JUST LET ME OUT OF THE CAR! PLEASE, OH GOD, PLEASE, LET ME OUT!!!!"

Fighting with every ounce of strength in my body, I managed to get the door open, falling out to the ground; I jumped up and ran harder that I ever have. Running down the hill, going around the curve crossing a small bridge, I saw a man on a tractor. When I heard the car coming behind me, I turned around and saw the faces of my attackers. Jake, who had been hiding on the back-seat floorboard threw my books at me as they ran me off the road. The man on the tractor saw them; he shut off his motor, yelling at me and asking if there was a problem. The car drove away at high speed. As I was picking up my books and papers, the farmer walked up to me wanting to help. I said, "No, I must go home. I'm okay."

While I was walking back to where we were supposed to turn, here comes Mr. Claymore with his carload. He stopped, asking me if something had happened. Looking straight at him, I gritted my teeth and shook my head no, but he knew something had. My worst fear was yet to come when I got home. The button on my plaid skirt was torn off, and my white blouse was wrinkled and dirty. "What am I going to tell her? WHAT?"

Mother was across the street visiting a neighbor when I got home. I ran to the house to change my clothes before she could get there, and brushed my hair. All she asked was had I been crying? I told her no, that it had been very hot at practice. I got busy doing the dishes and other things I had to do every day. There was never time for homework or for myself. That night as I lay in bed, I muffled my weeping. I was thinking back to when a man had tried to have sex with me when I was a tiny, nine-year-old child, then about my stepfather's friend that molested me for three years making me do things that I will never forget. I had managed to keep him from actually having intercourse with me by doing everything else he demanded me to do. When was this going to ever stop? For several days I convinced Mother that I was sick, so I could stay home from school. The fear of facing Mike and Jake at that time was more than I could handle. Jake had a really bad reputation; everyone knew not to mess with him.

Finally, the school called; on Monday, I had to return. After homeroom it was time for math class, then my biology class was upstairs. So I had to walk to the end of the hall to go up. Some one shoved me hard to the window, holding me tight. I felt a pain on the side of my neck. It was Jake, the one that had come up from the back seat of the car. He was growling as he said, "You ever tell anyone what we did, I'll slit your throat! You hear me Marion?" I could do nothing but nod my head while the other students just glanced and went up the stairs. He let go of me. When I looked at him, he showed me his switchblade, and motioned he would cut my throat. Of course I was late for class, but I never told anyone! Even when the teacher asked why blood was running down my neck. Mike never even looked at me for the rest of the year, not in school or in the band class. When was this going to stop! Is this what life is really about? What I didn't know was that the worst was yet to come!

Why Me?

Being trained at the age of five to take care of my baby twin sisters was fun until it became work every day. Before long, Lacy and Lynn were too big for me to rock in my little red rocker, not to mention I could no longer fit in the chair. Mother put them on her bed each day and told me I had to rock the bed on my hands and knees, so the babies would go to sleep. After they were asleep, I could slide off the bed, but Mother would lie on the other bed, and make me sit on the floor on my knees and fan her with a magazine. So many times I thought she was asleep, but the minute I stopped fanning, she would say, "Fan now." All I wanted was to go out and play. My only privilege was to go outside to the toilet. I remember I got to play a little during the few months we lived in Colorado. One other time I got to play when my family went to Florida to my step-dad's mother's house to show off his twins. Of course, I had to stay behind with a neighbor, but I did get to play and take a nap every day.

By the time I was nine, I was so tired of baby-sitting, but then Mother brought home a baby boy, Gary. Only one, not twins. I could deal with that. By the time he was one and a half, we were moving back and forth from up north. While there, I did get a pair of skates for Christmas. I waited and waited for the snow to go away. But before the end of summer, we moved back to home, and they made me give my skates away before we left. But I still had my brother. He lived in my arms until he turned 4 years old. He was fun to take care of. It felt like Gary was my baby, not Mother's, since she never had anything to do with him, or wouldn't. I could never understand why she would scream at me to keep him quiet, and then scream at me to put him down. Would I ever do anything right. She would make me go out with all three little ones while she cleaned house. We were not allowed to go back in until she said so, sometimes she would lock us out. If one of them got hurt, or left the yard, or broke something, I was punished. "Why do you hit me, Mother, for what they do?" She only gave me a hard stare.

One day Mother told me I was old enough to do the laundry alone. We had a wringer washer that sat out in the yard. You had to lay two straight-back ladder chairs down for the rinsing tubs. Then you had to carry buckets of water to fill the washer and tubs. Mother came out to separate the color clothes from the whites, telling me which to put in first. It was fun to do something besides taking care of the little ones and hanging the clothes out at the same time. I had watched her so many times, but she still showed me how to use the wringer, forgetting to show me how to pop the wringer.

The whites were finished washing, but you had to put your hand in to grab the sheets while the agitator whipped back and forth. Lynn came up and wanted to put a sheet into the wringer. I told her no, go away. She said, "I scream and tell Mother you hit me." I said, "Ok, ok, but don't put your fingers in it." Of course she did it her way, and her hand went into the wringer. I tried to get her hand out, just no way. I screamed for Mother, she and my step-dad ran out to pop the wringer. Mother was screaming, telling me I was so damn stupid that I would never grow up! Need I say I paid for that mistake? But I did finish the wash after the shock my mother received. I had taken my shoes off to keep them from getting wet. Every time I put my hand in the water, it shocked me. I ran into the house and told Mother. She said I just didn't want to finish the wash. She just didn't understand how much I enjoyed it. Out I went, trying to get the clothes out, but it shocked me again. Finally it hurt so much I had to get Mother to come out, with her threats of, "If it doesn't shock me, I'll beat you within an inch of your life!!!!" Of course, it didn't shock her. She just screamed for me to get it done! I went back in the house crying. I asked my step-dad to help me, because it hurt when I put my hands in the water. They both came out, cussing and fussing. Mother stomped over to the tubs and said, "See, it doesn't shock me. Marion's just a lying little bitch, and thinks she's not going to finish the wash." My step-dad said for me to put my hand in; crying, I did as I was told. I jerked my hand out, running to get away. He told mother to take off her shoes, then, put her hand in the water. Fussing, she did, and with a jerk, she screamed out more words than I knew how to spell! The second house from us had a short in their electric hot-water heater line that ran through our house. That was what the power company came up with. Mother never apologized.

Not long after, she told me I was old enough to clean house. My thoughts were that I could shut Mother and the little ones out, just like she did us when she cleaned the house. WRONG! You never locked Mother out. I paid for that one dearly. She said I had to take care of the three younger ones and clean house. I found out she was pregnant again, and she had to stay in bed until time for the baby. I was fifteen years old, taking care of my mother and three little ones who seemed to fight constantly. I felt lucky that the twins were in school most of the day, but at the same time I missed many days of school. People called constantly from my school, making threats if I didn't come back. To stop them from calling, I'd get to go once or twice a week. I would be so tired from cooking what was edible with Mother's commands, doing the laundry, cleaning, giving my siblings their baths, and helping the twins with their lessons and Gary crying for me to hold him. Plus my step-dad would make me go out for buckets of coal and make me chop wood. So many nights I remember going to sleep with my shoes and clothes on. One morning I still had on my coat. I was in junior high, and so tired that I forgot to brush my hair. I still had on the clothes from the day before. I could hear whispers and snickering. I was afraid to look; cringing just to get to class, I stared at the floor. "Can't anyone help me? Why can't someone help me?" I thought. "How can the girls in school be so neat and clean and smell so nice? When do they have time with all of the work?" Ashamed, I couldn't ask for help. How could I make myself look like them, and smell like them?

It came time for Mother to go to the hospital, so I stayed home to take care of Gary and see Lacy and Lynn off to school. There was the cooking, cleaning, and laundry, among other chores. An old lady in the neighborhood came to help me with the kitchen. Mother had a baby girl she named Sophie; my heart sank to my stomach. "Oh, God, please help me." The old lady, Mrs. Stanford, asked me, as we were doing the dishes, "Marion, aren't you proud your mother had a baby girl?" She saw the sadness in my eyes, tears rolling down my cheeks. She asked, "Girl, what is wrong? Talk to me." I broke down; "I just can't do it anymore Mrs. Stanford." I replied. "Not another one!" I told her about school, the work, and now another baby to take care of! "Please don't tell Mother, please???????" I knew what would happen if she did. She never said a word.

It was three weeks before I was allowed to go back to school. Spring was in the air. I knew without a doubt that I couldn't dress or smell like the other girls in school. But I could try. The day before, I found time to wash my hair, even if it was with the big brown bar of bath soap, took a good bath, and I rolled my hair with socks. I knew Mother had some deodorant on her dresser. I used it in hopes that my armpits wouldn't smell. But I didn't touch anything else. Big mistake! When I came home, she was waiting on me. She screamed and cussed me so much that I just couldn't take it anymore. I told her of the girls making fun of the way I smelled and looked. She didn't care! I was to never touch her things! I cried and told her, "It's not fair, I have to use the brown soap on my hair, and I have no deodorant, and no pads for my period. Why do you treat me this way, Mother? WHY???? Why can't I be like the other girls?" A slap to my face came with the screaming. She told me only whores used those things, screaming that I didn't deserve anything nice and that I needed to work harder. I thought of the sweet smelling Camay soap she used, her cologne, toilet water, and deodorant, and how she kept her hair fixed. Why was it wrong for me to use those things? What was I being punished for? All I wanted was to be clean.

With all the things that had been, and were, happening to me, no one, not even my Mother, could stop me from dreaming! Since I was 9 years old, I would climb the tree at the back of the house to hide and dream while lying on the roof staring at the stars. One day I'd travel and have my own babies. They would never be treated as I had been. Now with four little ones to take care of, the washing and ironing for seven people, it was impossible for me to even have time for my schoolwork. I shouldn't have worried, because the next year she made me quit school to do all of the work. Many things happened in the next several years that still make me ask: "WHY ME?"

First Born

Meeting a man that was so gorgeous that he looked like a replica of Elvis, my plans went into effect. Paul Heliconia, is the one I wanted to give me a baby girl, I broke my own rule; I fell in love with him, but I didn't want to marry him. Between him and my mother, I had no choice but to marry. Paul said he had us a place to live after we said our I Do's, but he lied. He moved me into his parents' house to be abused as a slave, and listen to filthy remarks said behind my back. Then we moved next door with his grandmother a few weeks later. Not long after that, Granny wanted to go back to her home in the next state with her daughters. I think she was quite senile, because of the unexplained things she did. But my mother continued to call for me to come and clean her house and yard. Being the obedient daughter I did what I was told.

The next few months passed quickly, then one night my back began to hurt. I woke my Paul, telling him the pain was getting worse. So what did he do? He shaved, got dressed as if he were going to a party, and went next door to get his mother! I tried to get off of the bed; it was impossible! Fifteen minutes later, he came back with his mom. Today, I wonder if he would have carried me to the hospital that night if she had not been there. She called my mother to meet us at the hospital. The next thing I knew Mother was standing beside me as the nurse was pushing on my stomach. I remember saying: "Stop, you'll hurt my baby." Mother's laugh made me open my eyes. She told me I'd had a baby girl. The next day, I went to Mother's house to the tiny room that used to be mine. Paul would bring his jeans for me to iron the day after our daughter Casey was born. They had to be creased and ironed to perfection. My thoughts were to tell Mother that I didn't want to go home with him, but I didn't. Two weeks later, Mother said I had to leave. Quoting her: "Once you leave the nest, you can never come back." I thought of Lacy and Lynn. Lacy had a big wedding of which I wasn't invited to; then my step-dad built a studio-type apartment for the other Lynn. They never had to do the laundry, or any of the chores that took up my childhood life. What made them so different from me? Both of them had come back home so many times.

Feeling scared to go to my own home was the warning that just added more worries. All of my groceries were gone. There was nothing to cook or eat, and crying seemed to be an everyday thing. My husband's sister-in-law, Kattie, came to see the baby. She told me that Paul's mother had taken all of the groceries and said she made sure that I wouldn't come back. That's why she treated me the way she had. His mom and dad didn't stop. It continued on, the lies and doing things to cause us trouble. We didn't have a washing machine, so I had to wash our clothes and the baby's diapers in the bathtub. His mom came down one day after he got home from work. She wanted to know what I was doing. After his answer of me washing clothes in the tub, she said there was no sense in that. I could use her washer. So a few days later, I did. She put the clothes in the washer, added my soap, and turned it on. She told me they would be finished in 30 minutes. I went home to clean some more, then returned later to collect my clothes. She then put my pre-washed diapers in the washer. When I finished hanging out the clothes, I thought, well, since she's being so nice, I'll visit her for a while. I picked Casey up and walked next door. My husband's sister, Annie had arrived without my knowledge. As I walked in the back door, the washer still had a while to go. As I walked towards her living room, I could hear Paul's mom saying, "She's tearing up my damn washer." Annie asked, "What did you say?" Her mom repeated, "She's tearing up my damn washer!" Then I heard Annie ask, "Who are you talking about?" My mother-in-law said, "That one down there, that thing my son is married to!" I had never touched her washer until now. I turned and walked back to the washer. Standing there with tears flowing, I thought, "Why is she saying those things that are not true?" I just shut her washer off, pulled out the wet diapers, and tossed them in the basket. When I got home, I put them in the bathtub to finish them. Paul's mom came down after he came home, wanting to know what happened. He said, "She won't tell me!" He then asked her what was said. She lied and said nothing that she knew of. Why tell him? He wouldn't believe me. One day when he came home from work while we were still living with her, I had worked all day doing all she told me to do. I had just finished folding the last of the sheets when I heard Paul pull in the driveway. I was barefooted and walked through the living room to tell his mom he was home when I went into shock. There she stood with all of the stove eyes on leaning over them. What is she doing? I sucked in my breath and backed up where she couldn't see me when she turned around. When Paul came in she had walked towards the living room reaching for her cigarettes on the television. I'm still in shock, she was all sweaty and red. Paul said, Mother, what's wrong, you look tired. She sounded angry telling him she had worked her ass off all day. He grabbed me by the arm hurting me, I said stop! He dragged me into the bedroom then shoving me in the room, asking why had I not helped his mother? Just because you're a fat cow doesn't mean you can just sit on your ass and do nothing! I told him what she did all day talking to the neighbors, saying nasty things behind my back while I did all of the work, listing it in detail. He screamed, "You're a liar! My mother works hard and would never say those things about you!" I told him to go and ask the neighbors that were here. In his eyes, his mother never told a lie, stole anything or mistreated anyone, but I knew all of those things were true. So, why tell him what she said about the washer.

Every day, one parent would be waiting for him when he came in from work, calling him to their house, knowing I had dinner on the table. Months later, I was very sick with a cold. I knew I heard his car, so I set the table for us to eat. An hour later, I bundled my baby and walked up to his mom's. Paul was lying on the floor in front of the heater, asleep. I bumped him with my foot to wake him, but his mom and dad said: "Leave him alone, he is sick!" As he woke up, I told him to come to the house and get his clothes. He asked, "Why?" I said, "Well, you spend more time with your parents than you do with your own family. So come get your clothes." I told him, "You are the one who wants dinner as soon as you get off from work, but you don't come home to eat. I cook your meals, wash your clothes, and clean your house. But you spend every waking moment with your parents. Maybe you're not ready for a family." He came home, and not much was said after that.

A few weeks after that, Casey cried until morning. I knew from past experience that this happened sometimes with colic. She finally fell asleep that next morning. Paul told me to stay in bed and get some sleep. Then I heard a knock on the door, his dad. I tried to go to sleep while listening to them talk. Then his dad asked him, "Why are you cooking your own breakfast? Where is she, still piled up on her fat ass? I'd tell her to get out here and fix my food. It's her place, not yours!" Paul explained about the night I had had. Then his dad said, "Oh, I didn't know that." Oh no, he woke Casey; up I came, angry and so tired. I stood at the kitchen door, holding my crying baby, staring at my husband with hot tears rolling down my face. A few months later, we moved around the corner from his parents. They were obsessed with being at our door every morning and night! At least, it wasn't right next-door.

Casey had caught the chicken pox from the little boy next door right before her first birthday, so she and I celebrated her birthday alone. Where Paul was, I have no idea. Since we had moved he never came home until the middle of the night. Later we decided to have another child, I must have been out of my mind or delirious. I told my husband I wanted ten children, just to be surrounded by love. But he was very seldom at home. It was a fact that some nights he couldn't find where I had moved the bed. Never going to sleep until he came home, I lay there and watched as he tried to get into bed on the dresser. He was so angry with me when I told him he should be at home with his family, instead of acting like he was single. I really wondered when did he have time to get me pregnant?

We moved again to get away from his family, after I proved his mother was abusing Casey with hard slaps. During my pregnancy, Paul took up racoon hunting. He never came home till nearly daylight. I did the gardening, tree and hedge trimming, and took care of his 20 hounds. I also took care of a German Shepherd that was a God—send, a pig that kept getting out, 2 cats, and 25 white chickens. Paul had run off all of the friends that I had before I met him. He'd called them names, which caused them to not visit again. He never allowed me to leave the house or yard. The baby inside of me could feel the stress, and she kicked constantly. She only let me sleep at thirty-minute intervals. Without a doubt, my baby was another girl. My husband would not accept it; he said I'd better have a boy, if I knew what was good for me.

One morning Paul walked in about 3:30, wanting to know what I was doing still up. I told him the baby was so restless that she was kicking hard. He sat next to me, and I took his hand, laying it where he could feel our baby kicking. He jerked away from me so hard, shrieking, "What is that?" I told him it was the baby. He told me I was sick if I thought he would believe such a thing. I was crying my eyes out as I listened to him going to bed. Daylight came, every morning I'd make coffee, homemade buttermilk biscuits, oats, and bacon. I'd wake him up for work; as he ate, I'd take my pans to the garden to retrieve vegetables for our lunch and supper. From 6:30 a.m. till 12:00, my work consisted of doing dishes, cooking, dressing and feeding our daughter, doing laundry, feeding all the animals, the yard work, hoeing the garden and doing the housework. And I still managed to present a nice, home-cooked lunch. He'd be home at twelve to eat. Each day I'd take different vegetables, so as not to eat the exact same thing every day. I learned how to bake, broil, fry, and burn food. I had no idea of how to cook his mom's way. Paul's family ate things that I had never heard of. It wasn't easy, but with practice in the years to come, I managed to become a good cook, farmer, animal trainer, baby sitter, artist, cake decorator and imprisoned slave. Without ever realizing it, I just moved from one abusing prison to another. But I really thought that was how life was supposed to be.

When the German Shepherd, Sasha, was given to us, she was for my little girl. I told the lady that I would train the dog to guard and protect Casey. I also told her that when I was finished, the dog would not cross the perimeter of our property. She said it was impossible to train a dog like that. I told her to watch in the months to come. My word was my honor. The dog stayed right beside Casey everywhere she went outside, never letting her cross the perimeter.

On August 23rd, 1968, I went into the house to get a pail of soapy water to scrub the porch. It was a good time, since Casey and her friend, the Shepherd, were playing. It would only take a second. On returning to the porch with the pail of hot sudsy water, I checked on my daughter and her companion. All was okay, with the two roaming around together. Watching them, I was thinking, soon she'd be two years old. She seemed to be more grown than she should be. The last time I tried to rock her in my lap, I was singing to her as I rocked. Suddenly, she looked up at me. By the expression on her face, you could tell she had something on her mind. Then she politely said, "Mommy, I think I am too big to sit on your lap now." Sliding down, she reached for the screen door: "I'll lie on the couch and take a nap. I'm a big girl now." She reached up to hug me, planting her little lips on my cheek. I sat there, rubbing my big stomach, thinking of my next daughter.

I went to the door to check on Casey; sure enough, she lay sound asleep on the couch. How long could I protect her from the things I never wanted her to learn or fear from the outside world? How could I guide my sweet little girl in the direction of a better life than we were having?

As I was scrubbing the porch, a bark brought me back to the present. The barking sounded as if they were on the backside of the house; Sasha probably saw a mouse or something. They were nowhere in sight. Panic hit my chest! I could hear the dog barking, and my little girl's screams echoing! Where are they? Holding my huge stomach, running as hard as I could, I thought, "The driveway, it's the only place they can be!" Every unimaginable horror went through my mind as I ran. I thought, "A car has hit my baby; Sasha has attacked her," remembering the previous dog owner's child being attacked after I told her not to let him roam past the perimeter. "No!!! She wouldn't attack my baby; it has to be a car. Oh, God, help me get to her!!!!! Please, let her be okay!!!!!!!!!" As I got around the curve to the straight-away, I could see them. I tried to run faster. "Oh, God, the dog is attacking her!!!!!! NO!!!!! NO!!!! SCREAMING AS LOUD AS I COULD!!!" When I got closer to them, I fell to my knees, crying with relief, knowing my first-born wasn't hurt. The dog let go of her sweater. The well-trained, loving dog had stopped my baby from going out into the street. A neighbor yelled and said that dog just saved your baby's life! I hugged the Shepherd, telling her, "Thank you so much, Sasha!" Why I did the next thing, I'll never know. I picked my daughter up and ran all the way back to the house. When I put her down inside the house, I latched the door where she couldn't get out. The pain of pains began.

Baby Girl

Thinking back to when I carried my first-born, I explained to Paul that it would be a beautiful baby girl. He said there was no way I could know. Waiting for my second baby girl, he wouldn't have it any other way; it had to be a boy! I was in turmoil the whole time I was pregnant, trying to prepare him for the fact that it was a girl. He kept warning me that I'd better have a boy. God knew I didn't want a boy! Most of the time, Paul stayed away from home, only coming back in the early morning hours.

As I stood at the latched door, my stomach and back were hurting so bad. Oh no, I knew those pains, and it was only one-thirty, still a couple of hours before Paul would be home. The thing I knew was to get Casey's clothes packed, since she would stay with my mother. Hoping Mother would keep her since I was going to the hospital. I hated to leave her there, but I had no choice. I bathed Casey and myself, while preparing her for what was to come. Telling her she must be a good girl, and when Mommy came home, she would have a little baby sister. Being excited about her baby sister, she was raring to get ready.

We were ready at 3:30 when Paul came in; I told him I needed to go to the hospital. Our first-born was so excited, telling him she wanted to go to Grandmother's house, so I could go get her a baby sister for her to play with. My husband didn't like that at all, and told her she would have a baby brother. Shaking my head, I asked him to please not say that; I knew it was a girl. Furious, he asked, "Where's my supper? You're not going anyplace until I eat." What else could I do? I held my stomach, trying to get his supper, every few minutes doubling up in pain. Then, after that, he said I had to clean the kitchen. He played with Casey, then, took his bath. I waited and waited. Later, we argued as I begged him to help me. I told him, "If you won't take me to the hospital, then will you please take me to my mother's house? Paul, PLEASE!" About ten-thirty p.m., he said he'd take me, just to get me to shut up!!!! Finally, in the car, I was holding the bottom of my stomach, and crying. He started in again in a mocking girlish voice; "We're getting closer to YOUR MOTHER'S house, getting any better? You ready to go back home?" Every two or three minutes all the way he repeated the same thing over and over. By the time we got there, the pains were getting closer together. I got Casey and her clothes, telling him to go away; I didn't need him anymore. Later, I found out that I would need him. I never dreamed my own mother would not take me to have my baby. She never did anything for me anyway; why had I expected her to help me now?

She came out of her house, asking what the hell was going on, as I sat down in the old metal bouncing chair. My husband, passing by to go inside, said, "Oh, she thinks she's having the baby." Mother came over to sit in a swing next to me, asking, "What makes you think it's time Marion?" I told her everything. We sat there until twelve-thirty, until the pains were very close and making me sick. "Mother, will you please take me to the hospital?" Her reply was like another slap to my face, "Hell no, I won't!" She went to the door to call Paul, telling him he needed to take me on to the hospital. He asked if she was going; same reply, "Hell no, I told you both I'd go with the first one, but your mother had to go with the second one." Mother told Paul to call his mother, so she'd have time to get ready. But he left me there to go for her. I couldn't believe anything that was happening. Why did these people hate me so much?

I can still feel the grip of the metal chair in my hands, as my fingernails began chipping with each pain in my stomach. Where is he? It seemed like an eternity before he got back. Finally, his mother walked up with her hand on her hip, saying, "WELL, are you going or not? I had to get out of bed to come over here!" I walked to the car alone. Of all things, they made me ride in the middle, because his mom didn't want to ride in the back seat. Paul told me to scoot next to him if I knew what was good for me. I had such a bad feeling. He drove as fast as he could over the railroad tracks. I gripped his leg when the severe pain hit so hard. He slapped my hand off, telling me not to do that shit again, or I'd be sorry. They talked to each other as if I were invisible. My thoughts scared me: "My mother doesn't love me, and I'm sitting between two more who don't love me." Looking down at my big stomach and rubbing it, I thought, "My baby will love me! I will have two little girls who will always love me." I just knew I'd never feel unloved again.

Finally at the hospital, Paul parked down at the bottom the hill, not letting me out at the door. How could he? I doubled up with pain inside the door; a black man who had brought his wife to the emergency room pushed a wheelchair to me. Paul told him, "There's nothing wrong with her; she can walk." He and his mother laughed out loud. The man asked if that was the father of my baby, as he helped me into the chair. The pains were so horrible I couldn't answer, only tears flowing. My thoughts were if I could get past those double doors, the pain would stop. Oh God! How wrong could I ever have been?

As I look back to that night, maybe I would have been better off to stay at home. In my wildest dreams, the horror of this delivery would have never entered my mind. People I didn't even know let me suffer. What was the purpose? Why? Even today, I still don't have the answers. I kept asking for Dr. Daniels, my doctor. The nurse said he was on his way, that there was plenty of time. You know how you can see the meanness in some people? The next nurse scared me as soon as she walked in. She asked me what I was waiting on. "Get your clothes off and put the hospital gown on, then get on the bed." I just couldn't be still, because the pain was so unbearable! When the nurse came back in, I asked if I could have something for pain. She told me, after the examination we would see, then she left the room. Oh Lord, here she came back with an enema. I kept quiet as long as I could then I told her it was running out on the bed, that she needed to stop. "Well," she said, "maybe you shouldn't have come in here with your bowels so full." I begged her to stop. There was no way that full bottle could go in there. The pains were getting worse and closer together. "Please, may I go to the bathroom?" Oh God, she finally stopped, telling me to go and do my business. But I was to come straight back! I did, and she was waiting with gloves on; now what? I could not believe what happened next. It felt like she rammed a hammer into my rectum. The pain caused me to scream at the top of my lungs. It felt like my back broke. I could hardly hear what she said, but I understood. No, I couldn't have anything for pain, but she wanted me to get up and walk around, saying I had not dilated enough to be there, so get up and walk.

I went to the waiting room to tell Paul what the nurse said, hoping to receive comfort of some kind. He wanted to know what I was doing out there. Without giving me time to say anything, he demanded for me to get in there and finish having that baby! He didn't want to see me again until it was over with. Why, why was he treating me that way? Shaking, I walked back, afraid to see the nurse, and unable to talk to my husband. "Oh God, help me. Let me die, so the hell around me will go away! Take my Angels and give them a good home, where they won't feel like I do! Where they will know life should not be this way; they deserve so much better."

Not long after that, I began to believe I really was in hell. I could hear two other women screaming down the hall. I balled up, holding my belly, so afraid of what would happen next. Why was it like this? What was going on? I tried so hard to call the nurse, the pains were making me sick, and they were getting strong enough to make me pass out. The next thing I remember was waking up, vomiting as I banged my head against the rails on the bed. I tried to call the nurse again; I knew she had to be close by, for the rails to be up. No one would answer me. The screams, the vomiting, the pains!!!!!!!!!! The nurse came back, with rubber gloves and demands. I asked her if Paul could come in there, he needed to be there. She said, "No! Besides, he and the woman he's with went out for coffee. They'll be back in a couple of hours." "May I have something for pain?" I asked. "No!" "May I have some water to get the vomit out of my mouth?" "NO!" I started screaming for Paul, but not for help. How I hated him for the way he treated me; how I hated working every minute. How I hated being his wife. "I'm not even your wife! I'm your prisoner!!!!!!!!!! I HATE YOU!! I HATE YOU!!! I'LL KILL YOU WHEN I GET OUT OF HERE!!!" The nurse said, "Don't you get it? He's gone. He can't hear you!" She put up the railing on the bed and walked out, as I was shaking from the sobbing. "Oh God, please help me," I begged. When the nurse came back, I asked about my doctor again. "Please tell him I need to see him, please!" She said he had more to do than to baby-sit me; with that, she left the room, saying I wasn't the only one having a baby. It wasn't this way with my first-born. What was going on?

Between screaming for help and vomiting, I finally passed out again. When I came to, the room was very bright with lights; they had moved me. A different nurse was standing there. I told her I needed to go to the bathroom. Right off the bat, she told me that I didn't have to go; it was just the pressure from the baby. I begged and pleaded with her to let me go. I can't hold it any longer, please let me go. She said if I thought I needed to go, she'd put a bedpan under me. The pan was so cold so I couldn't do anything. She said, "See, I told you." I begged and pleaded, trying not to mess up the bed. At some point, she had me strapped down so I couldn't get up. I would gag and cough from crying so hard; at least she wiped my nose. I was jerking, trying to hold my bowels back, pleading. She said she knew what she was talking about, and that it was just the pressure of the baby. Then she said, "If you think you have to go, then do it. If you do mess the bed, I'll clean it up." I kept saying, "Please let me up." "No, you can't get up, it might hurt the baby! Push if you need to!" I looked at her, saying I can't hold it any longer! My bowels let loose, and she said, "Oh, my God, you did need to go!" As she was pulling the sheets from under me, I asked for my doctor. "He is here," she said. When he came in, I couldn't see his face with the surgical mask on as he washed his hands. I asked Dr. Daniels if he could give me something for pain. No, in a while they'd give me something. What in the hell was going on? Why wouldn't anyone help me? The pains were cutting into my belly and back like a knife, so much that I passed out. When I woke up, the nurse was slapping my face. "Wake up; you can't go to sleep now!" I begged her, "Please give me something for pain, please!!!!!" The doctor came towards me. I had begged so much that my pains turned into anger. I screamed out: "If you don't give me something for pain, I'll get you if it's the last thing I do on this earth!!" I kept working with the straps as the nurse came around my head to my left. I grabbed her on the butt, clinching as hard as I could. She screamed at the doctor, "She's got me!!!!!!!!!!!" He came running up as my left foot came loose. I screamed at him, "You lying son-of-a-bitch, you're not my doctor!!!!" I drew back my foot and kicked him right in his privates, so hard that he flew in the air across the room, holding himself between his legs, and vomiting when he hit the floor. I tried to get my other hand and foot loose. Great timing; a pain hit so hard I welcomed the comfort of passing out. The nurse brought me to again by slapping me. I told her to stop it! If she only knew how many times my mother has slapped me! When I looked, they had strapped my left hand and foot so tight I couldn't move. The grit and pieces of teeth in my mouth told me I had broken several of them. The doctor had removed his surgical mask. He stood there sneering, with a dirty grin on his face, saying, "You will never forget this birth; I'm going to make you pay dearly for what you did." Screaming, choking, begging, I asked, "Where is Dr. Daniels?????" The doctor was very angry with me, saying, "Oh, you really want to know? He's on a yacht vacationing in the Caribbean. Did you really think he'd come all the way back here to deliver your baby?" With that, he and the nurse laughed.

My whole body started jerking, as if I were having seizures. Even today I can still see that doctor before my eyes: the white cap, hanging mask, glasses, and his white coat, with one arm crossed to the other elbow, one hand on his chin, and his index finger across his top lip. I stared at him until I passed out from the pain again. The nurse woke me again with the slaps, and the pains were worse than ever. I screamed for God to kill me, to let me die! I could see that doctor standing there as he watched my baby coming out, and I passed out again. I opened my eyes and he picked up something the light was reflecting off of it. Something cold touched my face as I opened my eyes. The nurse had put a plastic mask over my nose and mouth. She said, "Honey it's over now, just breathe." Thank God," was all I could mumble from my mouth. It sounded as if it was coming from another person. My eyes closed as the last thought entered my mind, "Now I can die."

But I didn't; I woke up asking myself if that was a horrible nightmare. No one was in the room with me, not even Paul. I needed to go to the bathroom. Pushing the button for a nurse, as she entered, I asked if I might go to the bathroom. "Well, of course," she responded, and left. I tried to get up, but my left side was so heavy it felt like dead weight. With my right foot and hand, I threw the covers back. It all came back like a flash of lightning. Oh God, what had they done? My hand and foot were black; they had cut off the circulation. You could even see bruises the straps left. What was I going to do? Not long after that, the same nurse came in, saying, "I see you made it to the bathroom." "No, I haven't; I can't get up." I kicked the covers so she could see why. A concerned look appeared on her face as she helped me. Finishing in the bathroom, I tried to stand up, but I hit the buzzer on the wall and fell on the floor. As I tried to get up, the door flew open. Another nurse asked, "What are you doing? What do you want?" I looked at her, saying nothing. She said: "Get up and go back to bed. You act as if you're the only woman to ever have a baby!" I did the best I could, with blood pouring everywhere from the bathroom to the bed. A nurse's aide came in to clean it up. I said I was sorry, and cried till a few minutes before eleven a.m. Right after the doctor came in, my thought was just let me go home. Three other women were brought into the room by then. The doctor and nurse stopped and spoke with the first one and second one; I cringed as he got close to my bed. He pointed from the foot of my bed and said, "She has to stay!!!!" Everyone went home except me, they left. I cried as hard as I did in the delivery room. A short, chubby woman brought a cold, wet cloth to me. That precious little lady came later with a coke. I asked her why I couldn't go home. She promised to see if she could find out why.

That night, the nurse came in to tell me I could see my baby. I was so tired that I asked her to wait. Paul came also; he wouldn't even look at me. He stood at the window, and said the only reason he was there was because his boss told him his place is to be with me. Other than that, he would not be there. The tears flowed like running faucets. I asked him what did I do wrong? What was I to do? He said he didn't care what I did. I asked if he wanted a divorce. He said maybe, he didn't know. I asked him, "Do you want me to give her up?" Again, he said he didn't care what I did with her. He left without a word. How could he, how? After what I've been through, how could he reject our baby girl? She had a hard time, just as I.

That night they brought my precious; with the state of mind I was in, I was afraid to hold her. Everything just kept running through my mind.

Was I dreaming somewhere in a coma, or was all of this real? The nurse was talking to me, and then to my baby. She brought her over and I turned away. A few minutes later she came back. Then she flopped my baby in my arms and said, "Now that is better." I looked at my precious little one who did not want to come into the world. "How could your father not want you, how?" I asked the nurse why was one side of her face so dark as if it was bruised. She said, "The doctor had to use forceps on her; she just didn't want to enter this cold place. From what I heard, she came into this old world screaming and kicking." I remembered when she was born, seeing the light reflection, but that wasn't forceps, I tried to tell the nurse, but what was the use; my baby is here now, safe with me, my little Sonja.

As the nurse reached the door, she turned to me and said, "That one's going to be a sassy one, yes she is!" I did the same with my newborn as I had done with my first. I counted her little fingers and toes, touched her little button nose, and felt of her dark, baby-soft hair. Hummm, she smelled so good. My baby girl was another beauty like the first. They told me the next morning I could go home, but the doctor didn't even bother to come in. The thought occurred to me, how? How were we to get home? The only thing I knew to do was call Paul's boss to pass on the message. He came, but ignored us. The only thing he said was: "Where are you going?" I said to my mother's house. As I walked to my mother's house from the car, there was my other daughter. She was so dirty; her hair had not been combed since I left. The same little ribbons were hanging from her little pony tails, all-lopsided.

One of the twin sisters, Lynn, had a baby just two weeks before, a little boy. My mother was busy getting a bed ready for me. With all of the noise in the hospital, I still had not had much sleep, and I was just so tired. My sister was standing beside me, saying, "Where am I supposed to go? You're taking my bed!" Her baby was screaming. I wondered what she meant, because I knew she had the studio apartment on the same property as my mother's house. The youngest sister, Sophie and little brother Gary were screaming and running like wild little Indians, playing. My mother was yelling for them to be quiet. I don't know why, but I started shaking, and felt like I was passing out. I had to get away. I couldn't deal with this now. I walked out, and asked Paul if he would please take me home. Please! He gathered up our things. In the car, I told him we would be better off at home. When we arrived, he helped me, to my surprise. Then I asked him to please give our oldest daughter a bath, bless her heart. I knew a dirty child was a healthy child, but it was ridiculous how nasty and smelly she was. Now my baby was sleeping, my first-born was clean, and we were home together, even my husband. We had some lunch, and he asked how I was going to take care of them, I needed to rest. Thinking about it, I told him if he could stay home the rest of the day, I could rest a little more. And then tomorrow I could just take it easy and do what was necessary. We all slept so well that night. Paul slipped out of bed to fix his breakfast. I needed to feel his arms around me, needed him to talk to me, anything. The only thing he said before he left was, "Go back to bed." He didn't even kiss me before he left for work. That's when I knew that it would never be the same again. It left me feeling so empty, as if numbness had seized my heart. No baby showers, no congratulations, no thank you, no one said anything to me. I finished my coffee; wishing one person would just hold me for a minute and let me cry out my sadness. There was no one who cared, no one. I walked to the bedroom where my babies lay sleeping. My little one, Sonja, was lying in the bassinet sleeping so peacefully, with her baby scent filling my lungs. "She loves me," I thought, as I put my hand on her little back. Touching her soft, dark hair, whispering, "It's going to be okay, baby girl. We had a hard start, so it's bound to get better for us now." She smacked her tiny lips, as if to let me know it would be okay. Then I went to look at my first-born, Casey. "She loves me too," I thought. "When she wakes up, she'll say it, as always her first words in the mornings. I don't need anyone; I have my two baby girls who will always love me! They will always hug me to remind me of their love, for the rest of my life! God, please give me the strength to protect and provide for my baby girls!"

Going Home!

Looking at my house, I wondered who had been there in the past couple of days, since everything was a mess. The broom in my hand was slowly sweeping as a car came up. It was Paul. I asked him why he came home. He said, "You're doing exactly what I thought you would." He had come home to take us to his mother's house. That's one place I never wanted to go, and I said that I would rather stay at home. He insisted! The first evening wasn't so bad. But the next morning, after he went to work, his mom woke me up, saying, "You can't lie in the bed all day. You have two kids to take care of." My daughters were both still asleep, and it wasn't even six-thirty yet. As always, I did as I was told. I got dressed, but there was no breakfast. She had started the dishes, and I had to dry and put them away. Paul's sister Annie, lived in a trailer in back of her parents' house. Banging the back screen, she came flying in to grab up my baby. I asked her to let her sleep as long as she would. She had to hold her, and she did all day. It didn't do any good for me to say it would make the baby sore. "Please put her down while she sleeps." She held her for the rest of the day.

Paul's mother wanted me to help her hang out the clothes, since I wasn't holding the baby. Later, we had lunch, and then did the dishes again. That night was horrible. My baby cried all night long. Bless her little heart, I knew she was sore from being held all day. The next morning I asked my husband to take me home; he said, "NO!" Not long after that, I had both of my daughters fed and dressed, and made the beds. Dishes again. The back door opened and slammed again. "Oh, there's my baby," Annie squealed out. Stopping her as she reached for my baby, I said, "Please, you made her so sore yesterday that she couldn't sleep last night for being in pain. So please, let her lie quietly on the bed." She ran through the house screaming for her mother. "Mother! She won't let me hold my baby!!!! Make her let me hold my baby!" Her mother replied, "That's her little brat, she can do what she wants with it!" Smiling, with tears running down my face, I watched my baby looking around, cooing at everything she could see. I whispered to her, "It's going to be okay, we'll be home soon." But it took nearly a week before I could get Paul to take us home. He finally agreed, after I told him that if I could be his mother's housekeeper, then I could take care of my own.

We all slept well in our own beds that night, even with the cramps starting up in my stomach. The next morning, I made Paul's breakfast. He asked if I felt okay. "Not really, just so tired," I said. He told me I was very pale, maybe I should lie back down while the girls were asleep. He would help me when he came home. Feeling worse, I didn't argue. Some time later my two-year-old woke me and said the baby was crying. I tried to get up, but I was so weak I couldn't make it. I put my hand in the bassinet with my baby; she hushed for a minute. I told my little girl where she could find something to eat. Later, I asked her to find some paper and a pencil for me. I knew I needed help in the worst way with my daughters. Writing a note, I instructed my two—year-old to take it to my landlady to call for help. Her house was right in front of our house so I knew Casey would be okay. When my little girl came back, she said, "Mrs. Crammer said she didn't have time to mess with you." What was I going to do? I needed help; I had no phone and no way to get up. I don't know if I kept passing out or what, because at times I couldn't hear the baby or the cartoons my daughter was watching. It felt as if I had wet the bed, so I put my hand under the covers to feel. When I pulled it out, it was covered in blood. I thought, "Oh, God, what am I going to do, I can't take care of my own daughters."

Paul came home and listened to Casey. "Mommy's still in bed, she can't get up." He came to the bedroom, screaming at me, "What the hell are you doing lying on your fat ass when you should be taking care of the kids and fixing my supper?" It took all of the strength I had to raise one leg and kick the covers back. As soon as he saw the blood, his face turned a sickening gray. "Oh, God, I didn't know!" he said, as he helped me up to the bathroom. He picked up the baby to see if she would stop crying. After cleaning myself, I went back to the bed, asking him to fix a bottle while I cleaned her. Then he bathed Casey after we ate supper. The only thing Paul knew how to fix was fried potatoes and bacon. Casey and I told him of the note and conversation she had with the old woman. He stayed around quite a bit after that, helping with different things. Sonja was two weeks old, and I still would get pale if I stayed up too long. Did it ever dawn on Paul to take me to the hospital?

One day in September, 1968, I'll never forget. My husband took over hanging the diapers and suggested that I go inside and lie down, since I was pale again. Later his brother, Seth had come to visit him while Paul worked on our car, which was interfering with the television. When Paul came in, I told him about it. He said he was finished, and that Casey was playing with his nephew, Sandy. About 15 minutes later, the television kept making a noise. I called out to Paul, no answer, but the interference just kept on. I walked out on the porch to see why he kept trying to start the car. I looked and the hood was up, but I couldn't see anyone. Then, to my left, Paul and Seth came from the backside of the house. Screaming, I asked, "Where is Casey?" Back to my right, our car was rolling backwards down the drive and I saw our little girl standing in the seat as his six-year old Sandy jumped from the car. I screamed, trying to run to the car, passing out before I could get to it. My husband ran pass me as I tried to get up. Paul said to stay down he'd get her! He did, and came back, saying Casey is ok as he helped me up. His brother just stood there, not offering to help me. I looked at the car up sideways on a bank. All that kept it from turning over was the opened door. My fists were clenching as Paul grabbed my hand, telling Seth he needed to leave. We were so lucky that we had taught our daughter to hold on to the back of the seat. She could have been killed when his nephew had put her up in the car; he had been the one trying to start it all along. I told Paul I felt so sick. He said I was as white as a ghost, and had blood all over my clothes. So I went in to change and lie back down. Finally, peace, quiet, and the slumber of wonderful sleep came to me. When I opened my eyes my husband was sitting in his chair. I got up and checked on my daughters, both sound asleep for the night. Then I walked into the living room. Paul wanted to know what I had on my mind. I looked at him, thinking how he had treated me for the past year, how hard it was to get him to take me to the hospital, when I needed help, not one person would. I told him we had two beautiful girls, and I loved them very much. "But please, never ever get me pregnant again." We never had any more babies!

Believe in Chain Letters?

More than 25 years ago, I heard about chain letters. If you received a letter with names on it, you dropped the first and added yours last, and mailed it to the recipients. Many said there was nothing to it, but others said if you broke the chain, bad things would happen. The first one I received, I participated in, and did as the instructions said. In due time, I seemed to forget it.

Then one day, another came to me. My work schedule, children, husband, and the small mini farm of 63 animals we had kept me very busy. Several times, I picked the letter up, not wanting to open it, because I could recognize it as a chain letter. So I tossed it into the trash Sunday night, thinking I just didn't have time for this silly mess. Monday morning, as usual, I put our laundry into the washer; it filled with water as I woke my girls to get ready for school. The washer stopped; nothing worked on it. Paul said he would look at it when he came home that afternoon. We all went our separate ways for the day, except for me. My car wouldn't start. I did all I could, even rolled it off of a hill. I called one of my co-workers, Jane to come for me; of course, she was late, which made us both late for work.

We had a very busy day, and with the changing of shifts, on my way out, something moved to my left. Well, of course, you'll look automatically.

My mouth flew open as I ran around a huge weaving machine to make certain that I really did see what I thought I saw. I really, really did! One of the weavers, Connie, who came to work more drunk than sober was urinating by one of her machines. As I stood there watching, she threw some cotton string to soak it up. Then she covered it with a stand-on box. I asked another of my co-workers what should I do? She said for me to report it right away. I did report it to the head supervisor, but he didn't believe me until the office sent a sample to the lab, and found out that it was urine, containing alcohol.

When I got home, I started my family's dinner. Putting the cornbread in the oven, only to find out later the bottom unit did not work. Oh well, what a day! Tuesday, still nothing was working. I went to work, only to find an angry Connie waiting for me with a pair of scissors in her hand, screaming and ranting about my report to the office. I told her she needed help in the worst way, and lying was no way out for what she did. If someone had turned her machine on, she would have definitely been killed. Connie kept coming at me, so I reached for my scissors; I wouldn't go down without protecting myself. Drunk or no drunk, you could smell the strong stench of whiskey on her breath. The office people came out and made her leave the building. Six weeks later, she fell asleep with a cigarette in her hand. She was so drunk that she never woke up while burning to death.

The same week, I found another woman's jeans and panties under my bed as I was cleaning. No one knew where the clothes came from. My oldest daughter, Casey, fell from a pine tree while using Paul's tree stand, skinning her chin and nose. My youngest daughter, Sonja, set the living room on fire while I was at the grocery store.

On Saturday, I helped Paul, by standing on crossties behind the tractor. He had turned the fields while they were wet. He yelled at me to drive the tractor and he would show me how it is supposed to be done, and that he could do it better than me. I tried to explain that you couldn't force them down because they would flip you under. Climbing on the tractor I told him if he wouldn't listen then hold on. When I looked back, he was under the ties, and I was dragging him on his knees. Stopping the tractor, I jumped off to help him. When he saw me trying to lift the crossties, he said for me to stop and go for help. I screamed, "Please, God! Please give me strength!" They were heavy, but I lifted both of them at the same time, as he pulled his legs out. Nothing was broken. When I found out he was okay, I said, "Well you can do it better than me!"

About two weeks later we went to his mothers house. She called me inside and asked, "What's this about you trying to kill my son?" "What are you talking about?" I asked. She explained what Paul had told her about the tractor. Then I explained what had happened. About that time Paul walked in, I don't know if I was angry, or hurt that he would lie to his mother. "Paul, why did you tell your mother I tried to kill you with the tractor? He looked so funny and said, "Mother, I thought you knew I was joking." She shook her head and Paul walked out. No wonder my in-laws think the worse of me. No telling what other kind of lies he had told them.

When we got home I looked for the letter! At some point, I had taken the letter out of the trash and laid it on a shelf. I opened it and continued the chain. All things returned to normal. I still ask myself, "Is there really anything to CHAIN LETTERS?"

The Thief That Got Away!

    Many years ago I did my large laundry items at a public laundry mat, always on Thursday. One particular time, as I drove closer to my house, I saw my husband sitting at the back door. I wondered why he was at home, that was strange; he never stayed out of work. When he saw me, he stood up. I knew it wasn't my husband, because this man was too short.

    I drove faster, and told my daughters to lie on the floorboard of the car and stay put. The man saw me turn into the driveway; he ran with his bag and jumped the fence. I tried to run over him, but at the woods I had to stop. I jumped out of my car, screaming for my daughters to stay put and lock the car doors. I ran after the man. As I entered the woods, I thought he might be sitting behind a bush waiting for me. I decided to call the police. It took three hours before a detective arrived. He did not take intruders fingerprints from the door he had entered; telling me it would do no good. The description I gave them was: 5'7" tall, 125 lbs, dark tan skin, black hair, and young, dressed in a dark blue uniform and carrying a half-moon bag. They did nothing! My thought, I'll do something myself! As I went out the door my daughter locked it. I went into the woods myself, standing in the most open area I could, looking around. Just maybe he dropped something. But, there were women's panties here and there on bushes, and I backed out of the woods. What if he was still waiting and watching for me? He had to be there when I called the police. The underwear wasn't there when I started in the first time.

I decided to call my mother and tell her what I had found. My brother Gary, his friend, and my sister came. We went into the woods with myself armed with a .38 pistol. There were panties all over the woods, even a pair of mine. Picking them up, I felt so violated. We found my husband's cigarettes that the man had stolen on the ground.

A few days later as I walked around the edge of the field, I found where the man had been sitting at the edge of the woods, smoking many cigarettes, mine and watching my house for hours or even days. A few days later, my husband said one of his uniforms was missing. We looked everywhere for it. So we figured the man that broke into our house took the uniform, since he had one on. By the end of the week we discovered other things missing: food, clothing, and so on. Not long after the story was passed around the neighborhood, other women started talking about their underwear missing. They were too embarrassed to call the police, since that was all the thief had taken. Several years later we heard the panty thief was still on the loose collecting panties. No one ever saw him, and he is yet to be found.

TELLING ALL!

In a hurry getting ready for work, I heard the phone ring. It was mother calling to say she had something very important to tell me before I went to work. I told her I'd be there in less than an hour. Usually I went each day when she called for me to spend an hour or so with her playing cards or dominoes. This time her voice sounded different. So off I went expecting coffee on the stove as usual. No cup, coffee pot cold. "Oh Lord, what have I done now? This is not good!" She was sitting at the table playing solitaire. As a rule, she always had my cards laid out or me. She didn't know that I knew she cheated, since I never said a thing to her. No cards for me today. I sat down, she said nothing, didn't even look at me.

My first thought was, "what have I done now?" I asked her, "What's up?" She kept playing cards. "Mother, have I done something wrong?" Not even looking up at me she said, "there's something I have to tell you before anyone else does." I said, "ok." Another thought came to me: she's going to tell me she knows something about my husband and another woman again. Not even close! Finally, she said that she and my step dad had gone to a lawyer the day before and made out their wills and that I'm not included. I sat waiting for more to come, nothing, so I said, "okay". Before I knew what happened, she jumped up, throwing the cards at me and hitting my breast, screaming, cussing, and shrieking at me! "Mother, what have I done?" She said, "I know my things aren't good enough for you". I asked, "Mother, what am I supposed to say? You never gave me anything in the past, so why should I expect anything now? You and daddy made it a point that neither of you ever wanted me! Anyway, the only thing I could ever want are the first wedding bands you had in the beginning." She bluntly told me she had already given them to me. I reminded her that she gave them to Lacy on her second marriage. She just stood there as if she couldn't remember.

At this point, I could feel as if something was wrong. She calmed down and asked me what made me think she didn't want me. I started when the twins were born, how she pushed me away, and how my step dad had changed because he had his twins now. He didn't want me anymore. "Remember after the twins were born while you were showing them off, people would ask who was I? Remember what he said: Oh she's not mine, that's her mistake. Do you know how that hurt me? You remember the little red rocker? I was five Mother, and I thought that you and Dad did love me! Then I learned that the chair was my prison until the two of you had to pry it off of my butt! Remember when you would make me get on my hands and knees on the bed between the twins and bounce them until they were asleep, then you would tell me to sit on the floor and fan you with a magazine? Remember you would never let me have friends or play with others? Why wasn't I allowed to play? Why did I have to work? I was five years old!!!!! Remember how I sneaked out one day and told the kids in the neighborhood that on Sunday you were giving me a birthday party? Remember what I did? I hid under the house where you couldn't reach me until Daddy came home four hours later, because you were going to beat me! All I wanted was to play like the other kids did!"

My mind was swirling with the past now, so I thought, why not tell all? "Mother, there are other things you should know! When your older daughter, Carmen, lived with us, the two of you left me with her boyfriend

Pat. He tried to have sex with me!!!! Remember how you dumped me off on the neighbors while you went to Florida? Remember how you made me stay with Daddy's army buddy Larry off and on for three years? He molested me!!!!! I begged and cried for you not to make me go with him!!!! I was a nine year old child!" She spoke up with, "why didn't you tell me then?" My voice was getting hoarse, but I told her what Larry said; "he told me that if I ever told you, that you would never believe me because even he could tell that you didn't want me, or love me, and that you would never believe me!" She just sat there staring into space. I continued. "Remember the people you sent me to Florida with when I was eleven? Their sixteen—year old daughter tried to kill me! Why? Because I was a good girl, I didn't ask for anything! You knew I had a toothache when you sent me with them! Mother! You never even met them, just sent me with a paper bag of clothes for Daddy to dump me off on those people! How could you? Because you hated me!!!!!" "You didn't want me!!!!!!" "Remember the church dance, the first time in my life I really got to do something nice? But when I came home, expecting you to be glad that I was okay after being in a four car pile-up, remember what you said when I came in? Oh! That's what you get for not keeping your ass at home! You didn't care if I was okay or not! I can still feel the pain I felt when you said that, it made me feel as if you wished I were DEAD!!!! Why? What did I ever do to you?" She just stared at me. My heart pounding, my hands shaking, when was I going to stop? My stomach was jerking as if I were going to throw up. But I couldn't stop, not yet! "Oh, there is more, Mother! I never told you about the boys at school that tried to rape me, but I got away. Only the first day back at school, one of them held the point of a switchblade to my throat and said he would slit it if I ever told. When the teacher asked why blood was on my throat, I just said I scratched myself. What they didn't know was that I was more afraid of what you'd do to me if you found out about it. I had no one to turn to! I'm not finished Mother! Remember making me quit school to clean house and be a mother to the four little ones? You told me I could continue school or quit, my choice. But when I got ready the first day, you cussed me like a dog, telling me that daddy couldn't afford for me to continue because he had four of his own that he wanted to graduate. You said he had supported me enough since I'm not his daughter and now I needed to pay him back for letting me live here! For letting me live here? I was a three and a half year old child when you married him! Why did I owe him? I worked for you and him every since the twins were born!!!! Remember dumping me at sixteen at that old woman's house where the fleas were eating me up and rats crawling on me at night? Remember when you and daddy took me three hundred miles away and signed me over to a man I had never dated? Remember you wouldn't send me $8.15 for a bus ticket, but demanded for me to come home? You didn't know that I sat in that hotel for three weeks alone with only one quart of milk and a small box of rice cereal. Have you ever drink clabbered milk? I did! I lost over thirty pounds from starving! Everything the two of you ever did was to show me how much you hated me!!!" I stopped, and she asked why I didn't tell her about these things when they happened? My heart was pounding so hard, and taking a deep breath, I replied with a question, "Would you ever have believed me? You never believed anything I told you." She whispered, "I should have given you away." Gritting my teeth, I asked, "Why didn't you? You never wanted me! There's one more thing Mother, the only thing I ever took from you in my life was a quarter when I was nine years old. Here's your quarter.

Remember after we moved back here? Remember how you held my hand over a red-hot stove eye trying to make me confess too stealing your change and cigarettes? Remember how you beat me until I wet my pants? Remember me begging you to stop hitting me?" Mother nodded her head yes. "Well I never took anything from you, but I took your punishment MOTHER!!! No mother should ever hate and torture their child as much as you have me! I'll never understand what I did so wrong." About that time my step dad came in the door from work. He said a very large cuss word and asked, "Are you still talking about that Marion? Why in the hell can't you let it go?" Mother jumped up and asked him what did he know about it? He had a smirk grin on his face and said, "Ah hell Francine, she never stole anything from you, it was me that took everything!" Laughing, he left the room. You could have knocked mother over with a feather; she was so pale it scared me. Thank God! She finally knew the truth. But I'll never understand the next thing she said so calmly to me, "It's time for you to leave Marion". I stared at her in disbelief. She screamed, "Get out! Get out! Don't you ever come back!" Hot tears were burning my face, wondering, "Why are you still punishing me for something I did not do?" Her screams brought me back, "GET OUT, DON'T YOU EVER COME BACK!!!!!!"

Over the next year or so I heard rumors that she was still talking about me, saying I wouldn't call or visit her. My friends knew me, and what she had said. I could never understand any of it. Then one day I heard she was sick. It made me wonder if she was pretending, since she had called more than a year before whispering she was having a heart attack and to come help her. I could barely hear her voice. I asked "Mother, is that you?" "Yes", she said, "Help, I'm dying." My heart was pounding in my ears. I ran to turn the stove off, jerking on my clothes. I was so afraid that I couldn't get there in time, driving like a maniac to her house. Finally I arrived, jumped out, leaving the car door open. Running so fast, I entered the house, screaming, "Mother! Mother! Where are you?" I heard her say, "Here I am in Sophie's room." Into my baby sister's room I ran. Mother was sitting on the side of the bed. I knelt down and asked if she was all right or should I call an ambulance? She threw her head back and laughed out so loud that it hurt my ears. I jumped up, confused, shaking my head, with tears swelling. "What's, what's going on, Mother? What? There's nothing wrong with you, why did you do that?" Her laughter finally slowed down enough for her to tell me that she must have had gas, and that she called me back, but I had left already. I stood there looking at her with tears running down her face, tears of joy for making me run, tears of joy for scaring me, tears of joy now that I'm late for work and my family's dinner not completed. "Mother, why did you call me? Why didn't you call a neighbor?" She never answered me, I left while she was still laughing. On my way home, I cried. Finally, getting the dinner done and on my way to work, I wondered why did she do me the way she did.

After she told me to get out for the last time, I didn't see her until she was on her death—bed. I knew if I didn't go see her that I would feel guilty the rest of my life, so I did what I felt was the right thing to do from my heart. Going to her, I sit the rest of the week beside her hospital bed. The last weeks of her life she spent at home, I did all I could to make her comfortable and happy. Feeding, bathing cooking and feeding her, I did her housework, laundry, and mine also before I went to work everyday. Everyone said she called my name over and over when I was gone. Twice I heard her screaming for me. When things would calm down, I asked her, "Mother, why didn't you ever love me?" She would close her eyes and sleep. As I stared at her, I thought of the seven other kids that she loved so dearly. All had turned their backs on her. I was the only one that made time to answer her beckoning calls . . . .

Where's the Beef?

The year could be 1976. We lived out to ourselves in the middle of a small forest area, but not too far from neighbors. There were plenty of woods and a 2-acre garden, with a large fenced-in yard. So, in no time, our little farm had accumulated a good selection of chickens, birds, geese, pigs, a couple of nubbin goats, a cow, and of course, a large selection of cats and dogs. With the price of beef going up, we decided it would be best if we bought a calf. Paul really took advantage of our fenced-in yard. Oh wow, just what I needed! At first, it seemed to go okay, except for one dog we had that was a Doberman.

During the summer, I would hang my laundry outside before I left for work. By the time I came home, all of my blue jeans were on the ground. I asked my daughters, Casey and Sonja and Paul if they knew who pulled my clothes off of the line. No, they didn't. My jeans were the only things on the ground. About two months later, I took Friday off from work. This gave me a little extra time to catch up on house cleaning, among other things. As usual, my laundry was the first thing to go out.

A friend called as I was cleaning the kitchen. Listening to her talking, I walked to the back door. There! So that's the one that was taking my jeans off of the line! It was the dog. He didn't tear them, but he walked back and forth under the lines pulling all of my jeans down. After I hung up the phone, I collected six pairs of jeans from the ground. He had always been a pretty good dog, but now, how could I stop him? I knew how to get a dog to stop eating chickens, but would it work with the jeans? I called Gambler; as usual he came running to me. When he got close, I took a pair of my wet jeans and tied them around his neck. Not too tight, but where he couldn't pull them off. Needless to say, I had no more problems with him. I guess he blamed me for the new big dog (calf) taking up his space in the yard.

The calf, Clementine, was growing like an unwanted weed. She watched our daughters go in and out of the gate. Being a smart girl, she learned to open it. Two hours later we would finally convince her to return to the yard. We hung a piece of tow chain on the inside of the gate and she wouldn't try to get out, just looked at it and went on about her business. One morning, I had stripped my beds for washing and hung my sheets outside. After work, I went out the door to get my laundry. All of the white sheets were dirty. What the blue blazes was going on??? I washed them again, but this time they went to the laundromat to dry, since it would soon be dark. The next time I hung them out, we went to the grocery store, came back, and the same thing again: dry, but dirty!

Paul told me after they were washed to hang them out again. We would stay close by and see how the sheets were getting so dirty. Okay, but they were going to be worn out just from so many washings! We were cutting grass and trimming the shrubbery, since it was Saturday. The bush hog stopped; I looked to see why, Paul was pointing at the laundry. We walked down to the lines quietly, watching. Clementine was blowing her nose on them, not on another thing, just my clean white sheets! I was so angry, I told my Paul it was time for her to go into the freezer! Of course, he wanted to wait a few more months. Why is it men never listen to women? I'll never understand.

About three weeks later, I was cleaning the yard. Casey and Sonja knew to always put the chain on the gate. Each time anyone went in or out, you could hear the thunder of Clementine's hoofs running to check it. As soon as she saw the chain, she would walk away and go back to her business of helping me keep the grass mowed. The girls had gone to a neighbor's house to ask if their daughters could come to play. Of course, here come five little girls. I walked around the corner of the house to clean the front porch as they were coming in the gate. I looked at the gate and screamed, "THE CHAIN! THE CHAIN!" Too late! Clementine opened the gate, and shot out like a bullet. She was running like a wild buck, kicking up her back heels as if she was saying, "Goody-goody, I got out!" She looked just like she was smiling at me.

Now between our driveway and the railroad tracks there were kudzu vines, which are very thick and about three to five feet high. Of course, she just disappeared as I yelled at the girls to open both gates. Could I have any luck with her? Walking, I went the way I last saw her, calling "Clementine, Clementine!" I couldn't find her anywhere. Of course, a train had to come by at that time. The engineer was blowing his horn, it sounded different than usual. Oh no! She wouldn't! She didn't! Trying to hop, jump, and run through the vines with my short legs was virtually impossible, but I managed to get on the bank to see the tracks. There she was, standing in the middle, looking at the train! I called her, knowing she was too stubborn to listen. The only thing I knew to do was to fall back on the vines. I was hoping if she couldn't see me, maybe she would at least get off of the tracks. It worked! In the meantime, she flew by me just inches from my head. Off we went again! I was up and running after her, my feet tangled in the vines, throwing me face down. If I'd had a gun, there would have been a big barbecue on that day! Believe me! One of my shoes disappeared in the vines when I fell. As I stood up, there she stood, mooing at me! My right foot was cut completely across the top, and bleeding, both arms were scratched from blackberry briars, tears' running down my face, and the cow was laughing at me! I can say this, it was a terrible situation, but she made it even worse by laughing at me! Talking to her, I thought maybe I could coax her into walking back to the gate on her own. Who was I kidding??? She mooed at me once more, then turned in the opposite direction and took off. I was still stuck in the vines and briars. When I got out, I kicked off my other shoe, running as hard as I could to catch up with her. Now we were in the other section of woods. I whistled and called, but nothing. Not a sign of her anywhere. Oops! There she is! Running to get behind her, in hopes that I could head her back to the gate, but she just disappeared. She was probably standing somewhere, laughing at me again. Then I heard my car. Oh, thank God! I whistled for Paul to stop. Now I had help. He got out of the car, and just started laughing. My blood started to boil! I asked him what did he see that was so funny? He said, "You should see yourself; what have you been doing?" "I'll tell you what I've been doing! For the last three-and-a-half hours I've been chasing that stupid cow! Now I can't find her! He just laughed that much harder. I got so angry! I told him if he had been the one chasing her, he wouldn't think it was so damn funny! "Now help me find her!" I shouted. He was laughing so hard he had to hold his stomach while pointing to the woods in front of me. I looked, and sure enough, there she was, standing and watching the show! My husband's laughter finally slowed. Out into the road I went to find the biggest rock I could throw; I missed her! "I'll kill that cow if it's the last thing I do!!!" He told me to get in the car and drive it to the house to block the drive, where Clementine couldn't get past it. "Oh! So you think you can drive her in the gate! Okay! Go for it!" Off to the house I went, thinking, "I really hope he has just as much fun as I did!"

I blocked the drive and set the gates, but where is he? I went in the front door, stopped in the kitchen for a cup of coffee and a cigarette, and went out the back door. I couldn't see him or the cow. So I sat down on the porch and waited. He yelled out, "When I catch you, I'll kill you!" I looked toward the woods where I heard him yelling, and there went the cow. WOW! Paul was up in the air going head first in a flip, landing on his back! I laughed so hard I wet my pants! Clementine galloped to the gate, came in the yard, and around the house she went. My husband was right behind her, yelling, "I'll kill you!" He had picked up a brick and threw it, knocking her down. My laughing was uncontrollable now. My husband looked at me as if he could kill me. "What do you think is so damn funny???"

No need to say he called the slaughterhouse to come for her the next day. They came, a man and three boys. They took a small rope, lassoed her, and tied her to a tree. Out the door I went screaming, "You can't leave her there, she'll pull that tree up!" The four of them could not get her out the GATE! They finally had to bring the truck inside and hem her up in a corner. It took them six hours to get one cow on their truck.

Our minds couldn't accept eating beef so it took us a while before we could eat dear old Clementine. One day, I was thinking about the time she laughed at me, and that did it! I called and invited everyone to a huge barbecue. Everyone that came through the gate hung the chain, and then asked, "Where's the beef?" With a huge smile on my face, I held up a thick juicy steak from the grill and yelled, "Come and get it!"

STRANGE NIGHTS

My family and I moved to our summerhouse in the country, where all was peaceful and quiet. Strange things happened in the night that many never saw. The ones that did said nothing, for fear of being thought of as mad. What really went on in the darkness of the night while many slept? I was the one person who couldn't sleep; I kept hearing sounds of roaring motors at 2:30 a.m. one morning. Looking in on Casey and Sonja before I went to investigate the sounds from outside. Going out the front door, I stood on the porch, wondering why the vehicles had their lights off. I was trying to get closer without being seen. Many military jeeps and trucks, bumper to bumper, filled with armed soldiers, were coming from a side road to the main highway. All of them were turning in the opposite direction from my house. It was so strange that I wondered what was going on? Were they in training or did they know something we didn't. In the house I changed into dark clothing to get a closer look at the convoy. Maybe I could hear some of them talking.

One soldier's jeep blocked the highway as he was directing the convoy, but there was no traffic that time of the morning. The brush at the edge of the field was high enough that they couldn't see me crawling on the ground. As I stared, my heart began to race. In fear that the one soldier standing would see me as he turned, I froze. "Please, God, don't let him see me." Something terrible was going on. If not, why were they driving with no lights at 2:30 a.m.? Why were so many soldiers heavily armed not saying one word? Training?

Never moving, only to breathe, my thoughts went back to three nights before, when I was sitting on the front steps smoking. I was gazing at the beautiful stars while being curious about the orange light on the mountain before me. The loud chopping noise had to be a helicopter. I ran across the lawn. It was coming from a friend's summerhouse around the corner, the same direction the soldiers were coming from now. The chopper, which had to be jet black, lifted without a light on. You couldn't see anything, but you could hear the sound of it going up. The next day I went to investigate the property. You could plainly see the indentations where the helicopter landed on the grass. I never could explain how it got there without me seeing or hearing it come in. As for the convoy, it was ending, and the last soldier left in his jeep. The next day I went to the community from the direction the convoy had come. Questioning several families that I knew along the country road, I asked had anyone heard the helicopter or seen the convoy? No one heard or saw a thing!

Not long after that, on a cool morning, I went out to hoe the garden of pesky weeds. The sun was shining, what a beautiful day! A couple of hours later it got very dark, and the wind came up so fast. Running to the house, I stopped and looked up. What was that? Was it a tornado? It was so scary with the clouds whirling in every direction. It looked like something from a sci-fi movie. I stood there looking up, and it just stopped and disappeared; then there was blue sky with sunshine again. Later I asked the neighbors about it, but they hadn't seen a thing! What is it with these people? Am I the only one seeing these things?

My daughter stayed home from school one day and it happened again, only with much harder winds. Dirt, among other debris was flying through the air. I screamed for her to run! She said, "Mom, what is wrong with you? It's just a little wind." I asked her if she saw what the clouds were doing. "It's just cloudy. Mom, calm down; you're as white as a ghost. What is wrong with you?" Did I imagine it twice, or was I the only one who could see it?

On an afternoon when I had picked the peas, I decided to shell them for dinner, big cowpeas. I was sitting on the front porch with my chair leaning against the house. Something caught my eye; thinking it was a buzzard or a hawk, I didn't pay much attention. It was an everyday thing, seeing birds flying around. Finally looking up, I thought, "Oh, good Lord!" It was the biggest camouflaged airplane I had ever seen. There was no sound whatsoever! It was right above the power lines, and I knew my camera was right inside of the door. Jumping up and running, I thought I would have time to get the photo! Less than 10 seconds later, I was standing in the yard with my camera in my hand. Where did it go? I ran in every direction! I ran out onto the highway to more open space! There was no plane in site! It just vanished! Of course, no one saw that either!

Not long after that, I was hanging clothes out to dry. Dropping the clothes, I had to cover my ears! It was so loud! Looking right above the trees, I saw a huge jet zoom over! The tall pines bent nearly double from the wind of the jet. The next time he came over, the whole house shook and the windows rattled, some of the panes in the windows cracked. Believe it or not, the neighbors did see this one! I asked if there was someone I could call, because the pilot was going to crash, I could feel it. They didn't know of anyone, I told them it was a boy in that jet and he was going to crash! About two weeks later, the neighbors asked me if I had heard about the pilot, he had crashed into the dam. Was there any way I could have stopped him? I don't think so.

Strange things do go on in this country!

CHRISTIAN

During my lifetime, I visited many different religions, from tent revivals to big churches. At times, I thought if I kept on, I would find the right one for me. Some of the things I saw at meetings would discourage me so much. So I started taking notes, and asked myself, "Is this really the way things are, or can there be another way. What is Christianity?" Along the way, I learned a few things.

At one of the first meetings I went to, a woman said there was someone in the audience who had a problem with their ear. As I looked around, as everyone else did, she walked right up to me. There was no way that lady could know I had a problem, unless the lady I arrived with told her. Even if she didn't know that a bug had entered my ear the week before, it was a horrible experience. When it happened, I went to my mother, where she lay sleeping. I whispered, but she couldn't hear me, so I touched her and she screamed out. I was crying and holding my ear, and she asked what was wrong. I told her of the bug buzzing in my ear. She put my head in her lap to see if she could see it. In the meantime, my stepfather was putting on his clothes to go to the neighbor to borrow some oil. He was hopping around, saying he had seen a man in Korea go crazy because of this problem. Mother was screaming at him to be quiet and go for the oil.

It had made me feel much worse, with the bug wiggling inside of my head. They put the oil in my ear and the bug finally got still.

Back to the meeting, they apparently thought I had an earache. Explaining that I didn't, she kept trying to pull me up to the front of the audience. Breaking her hold on me, I ran outside. About six weeks later, the bug eventually came out; it was a big one.

I went to church any time I could; it was the only place I was allowed to go, if I took my little brother and sisters. There would be so many questions in my head about God and Jesus. Many were never answered. Once, after I got older, I was allowed to walk to another tent revival. One of my classmates had painted my fingernails red Friday at school. Wanting to learn what these people could teach me, I sat right up front, eager to hear what they were saying. The preacher, who was shouting at the top of his lungs, made me wonder if God was that hard of hearing. All of a sudden, the preacher came to me, hitting me on the head with his bible, saying, "We must pray for this child, she is not a Christian!" Why was he saying that? I didn't understand. Then he said that I had the devil's color on my hands, and I would walk through the doors of hell. So everyone prayed for me. I watched some of the people from my neighborhood up in front, jumping up and down, jabbering in some language. One lady winked at me, and I knew she was pretending. Not long before, I had met a young man who had epilepsy, and I thought, oh, many of these people have it. I closed my eyes and said a prayer for them; they needed help worse than I did.

After the meeting, people were giving money, and many had brought canned food. While I was looking around, I saw a classmate from school. I asked him why they were giving money and food. He said that it was to pay the people that were on the stage. I asked if they were actors, he said no, just religious folks. It made me feel like something was wrong. As the people began leaving the meeting, I heard laughing from a trailer in the back. I asked my classmate Ed. if he would go with me to see what was going on; he did. The two of us stood outside and could hear them saying: "Boy, these people are stingy, but we got enough to go out for steaks." Another asked what they were going to do with all of the canned food. They were going to sell it in the next town. Someone came out before we could get away, and said that we were listening to their conversation. We ran hard. I told my mother about it, and she said that happened a lot. She always said there were more hypocrites in church than out, and that was why she would never go to church.

Later, I went to a church not far from home. When the preacher said good morning, one tiny old lady went into fits. She was saying something no one could understand, and was jumping up and down hard enough to jar the church. She asked me one Sunday morning to sit with her. She was nice, so I thought, why not? There came the preacher. POW! The tiny lady had jumped straight up and popped me right in the mouth, splitting my lip. With blood on my hand, I went home. Never again did I sit with her. But I wondered, was she that close to God, or was she pretending? I stopped going to that church, because I didn't like some of the things I saw going on. But I can say a few weeks later, the tiny lady jumped up and down one time too many, because a lamp from the ceiling fell right on top of her head. They said she behaved after that. My conclusion is that my question about her had been answered.

After awhile, I was allowed to go to another church, when the Elders talked mother into letting me go. It was very different from the other places. They did what they could to entertain the children, as they taught them about religion. But my questions still had not been answered. One Easter my mother made my three sisters, Lacy, Lynn, Sophie, and myself all dresses just alike. I felt so proud, because we looked so neat and clean. My little brother had on overalls with a white shirt and his little cap.

Mother had never been to the church, so she never knew we were the outcasts that Easter in church, and I'll never forget it. The women had on their new Easter bonnets, with matching suits and little white gloves. I had never heard them say anything bad about anyone until I brought my little sisters out of the bathroom. The women were around the corner talking about how ridiculous we looked. Tears stung my eyes. I grouped my sisters and little brother close to me. As the women entered the chapel, I stared at them. Was this what I was baptized for? My happiness faded, and my trust that this would be the one place no one would make fun of me, went down the drain. I stopped going, but the Elders wouldn't give up on me. There was to be a Green Ball in the big city, and I was invited to go. To this day, I don't know where my dress came from. It was a beautiful green chiffon semi-formal gown, and it flowed in the wind. I had on some beautiful little heels with my first hosiery. All the bad things that had happened to me just disappeared for a little while. My friend and classmate, Janet, loaned me personal things, and showed me how to shave my legs. It was so much fun, only it was fun that would end all too soon.

When we got to the city, the car behind us belonged to our group. The driver, Roy, a classmate of mine, was acting stupid. I saw it before it happened. I begged the Elders to stop, and make him quit! "Please make him stop! There's going to be a wreck!" They said not to worry it would be okay. I screamed, "No, it won't! There will be a wreck!" About that time, we were hit three hard times from the rear! I grabbed Janet as she was flying to the back window! The one behind hit us, we hit the one in front, and they hit the one in front of them. I looked around and there were three other cars wrecked. I helped Janet, but the Elders had the worst of it, with their knees bloody. One of them held out his hand to me. My hand reached out, but that was the last thing I remembered, until I woke up with a nun standing over me. I asked if I was in Heaven. "She said, "No, my child, you'll be all right. Everyone, she's awake!" The two Elders came and squatted in front of me, asking, "Marion, how did you know that was going to happen?" "I told you in the car! I saw it happen!" They looked at each other, and asked if I was okay. When I came home that night, I was excited to tell my mother what had happened, hoping she would be glad that I was okay. She said she had heard about it, and that was what I got for going in the first place when I should of kept my ass at home. She had no concern whatsoever for me. After that, the Elders never came for me again. I still don't know why, and they never answered my questions.

After my mother made me quit school she wanted me to go and live with a woman, Beth, who would pay me a dollar a day to stay with her while her husband travelled. On the first night Beth told me she had to go to church that night, and I had to go with her. It was fine with me; maybe it would be more interesting than the past ones I had been to. We got to the church, and her brother played the guitar while we all sang hymns. I sat there watching, while they started walking to the altar. They were all yelling and screaming at the same time. Some of them were even jumping up and down. Is this the way everyone talked to God? Beth had walked up to the front also. I just sat there fiddling with the buttons on my blouse. They got a little quieter; I saw Beth and her mother coming towards me, thinking they were going to sit down. Her mother told me to go to the altar and "REPENT YOUR SINS! YOU'LL GO TO HELL IF YOU DON'T! NOW GO AND REPENT!" I was shaking my head no, but Beth's mother and two other ladies grabbed me, pulling me to the altar. While I was trying to get away from them, they tore the buttons off of my blouse and tore my skirt. I was screaming "LET ME GO!" I ran as fast as I could out the door! I heard them screaming that I was a sinner, and God couldn't enter the house of the Lord with me in there. They said, "Don't come back in here until you REPENT, CHILD!" Beth came out, giving me her sweater to cover up, and we went back to her house. I never went back there for many years! I knew right from wrong, and had not broken the Ten Commandments. I obeyed my parents, and they told me to obey all adults. Why was I a sinner?

After I was married and had my two babies, another religion came into my life from the neighbors. I really enjoyed the way they studied the bible, it was so easy to learn things. Not long after, they told me I couldn't go to funerals, unless it was a way for my husband to feed us. That was worshiping the dead. I had to take all of my pictures of Jesus out of my house, it was wrong to have them. Then I had to go to a building that wasn't called another word for church. I only made it a couple of times. I was ordered to have my daughters asleep when they came for bible study, and at the building, they said I had no control over my baby. I explained it was to hot for her in there. They said I couldn't come back until I learned how to control my children. No one preached, just put on a show of how to have bible studies in the homes. They stopped coming to see me. They never answered my questions either.

A few years later, I had to go to the store one Sunday morning. A tire blew out on the car right in front of a small white church. Trying to change it myself proved to be more difficult than it should have been. A man parked his car and proceeded to help me. I told him he didn't have to since he was dressed up in a nice suit. He said he had not done his good deed for the day and this is the way our Lord reminded him. I thanked him and he said he was the preacher at the little church, and invited me to come for service. I told him I'd like to come to the night service, if that was okay. He said that it was a nondenominational church, and all were welcome. That night, I dressed my daughters, and we walked down to the church. Entering, I recognized several of the older folks. Introductions and greetings were made, and I went to the front pew to sit down. A few older ladies were grouped together talking. One said, "Why is she here? She's nothing but a whore!" I looked to see whom they were talking about; it was a young girl, Susie with her baby girl. When I was young I used to clean her mother's house, so I asked her to come and sit with me. Susie had heard what they said and wanted to leave, but I asked the ladies if all they came to the church for was to ridicule each person who came in the door, how could they call their selves Christians? Susie then came to sit with us. I never asked my question, and I never went back.

It was years later before I went to church again. Maybe it was time, since I lived in the country, where good, hard-working people lived. It was a small country church, but when you walked in, it seemed to be divided. One side wanted me to sit with them, and the other wanted me to sit with them. So I chose the middle. They asked me to join the Women's WMU church club. I agreed to go to one meeting. Everyone seemed so nice, and I felt as if I belonged. The meeting came to order and I was welcomed. Listening I watched to get an idea of what it was about. Then they questioned me, to see if I had any ideas of what the ladies could do during the long winter months. Many of them I had met the previous year. I suggested that each meeting take place at a different home of the ladies' each month. We could come with cakes and so on to eat, instead of one lady doing it all herself. Then they asked what we could do at these meetings. I suggested that each lady could teach us something she knew how to do. It seemed that all of the ladies had different talents. Everyone liked the ideas, I thought. It came time for the meeting to end and have coffee with cake. As I listened to the ladies, I noticed one group huddled together whispering. One was motioning for me. I walked over, and they said they wanted to talk to me. The two, Sharon and Dawn that lived close to me took me aside, and said they had never had anyone come in with so many ideas that is not a member of their church, or a Christian. I asked what were they trying to tell me. Then Sharon, the tall one, who already knew I had been baptized, said I had to be baptized or get out of their church! I told her that I didn't think that was the way it was supposed to be. Anyway, how was I supposed to get home? She said she would take me, and told the others she had to. I told her she needed to think about her definition of the word Christian. At that time, I didn't know if the other ladies knew what it was about or not.

Then came the time to do volunteer work at the church's second-hand shop. Of course, I was notified since the church still had me down as a member. The very two who didn't want me at church were the ones who came for me. When we got there, I asked what I should do. I got busy cleaning and folding clothes; then a customer came in and asked for my help. Sharon came over putting her hand on my shoulder, telling me I was not to help the customers, only to work. I thought that if I stayed busy, the time would pass, and much of the work would get done before the end of the day. Another customer asked me for help. I apologized and told him that they told me I couldn't help the customers, he asked why. Shaking my head, saying I don't know why. I went back to work, down on the floor on all fours with a hand brush, cleaning out from under the lower shelves. Someone say something, pushing my hair out of my face, I looked to my right and saw a nice pair of shoes, with dress pants above them. Ignoring him, I went back to work. He tapped me on the shoulder and said, "I'm talking to you." Standing up to hear what he said, I begged his pardon. He said, "I said if we had more Christians like you, many things would be accomplished." I could see Sharon and Dawn standing in the back, green with envy. The man held out his hand to me and I refused, because my hand was so dirty. He said, "I don't mind a little dirt from a hard-working Christian! Thank you!" Later I found out he was the leader of the whole southern religious organization. The two ladies really put me through it then, not speaking to me all the way home. Then, at my house, as I stepped out of the truck, Sharon slung gravel all over me. I think the man gave me part of the answer to my question.

A few months later, Sharon pulled up in front of my house, honking her horn. I went out to see what she needed. She said Dawn's mom had died, and since I was still on the membership list, it was my duty to share in the work. I asked her why I was not good enough for her church, but I was always good for the work? I looked at her and said, "Don't answer, but tell me how can I get to where the lady died?" She said she would pick me up and take me there. I got ready to go, and looking at what little food we had, I made a couple of dishes to take with me. Sharon came, and never said a word to me until we arrived. When we entered the house, she led the people to believe we were best friends. I asked her what was I to do? She told me in the kitchen that I was to work. I asked her if she was going to help me? No, she had to go home to cook for her family. I thought about my family, but I'd cross that bridge later.

Dirty dishes were everywhere; I cleaned and cleaned, never saying anything. It would be okay; I could do it. When I finished, I made coffee; there were two coffeepots. Setting out cups, saucers, napkins, and spoons on a serving tray. I asked everyone if they would like some coffee, cokes, or anything else. Then I noticed the folks outside. Sticking my head out, I asked if they would like coffee, and many said yes. I wrote down on my list how many coffees and so on. The people inside were in nice clothes; the people outside you could tell were not so fortunate. As I made a second round with the coffee pot, a man took it from me, handed it to his wife, and said with tears in his eyes: "I quit going to church because of the hypocrites." He said he was kin to every soul there, and many of them were bigots and back stabbers. I said, "Excuse me, but it's not my place to say what they are." He said, "Listen, you've made me see that you can be a Christian, even among the lot of them that are not." He continued, saying that I was the only real Christian in his deceased mother's house. I told him I didn't know if I was a Christian or not; that wasn't for me to decide. "What I am doing is the polite and respectful thing to do when a family is in need." I said, "Thank you for your kind words, but you must do what is right in your heart. More coffee?" He had not known that his sister, Dawn was one of the two that had told me to get out of the church.

As I entered the kitchen, I saw Dawn standing there, crying like a colicky baby. She reached out to me, and I backed away from her. Looking at her, I said, "Please don't touch me." She cried even harder as I sat the coffee pot down, I thought about what her brother had said, then turned around and let her hug me. She cried and said, "I am so sorry for what I did. I can't believe the only person I didn't want in my mother's house was the only person who came to help, not even my best friends came to help." Maybe I was wrong, but I felt no sympathy for her whatsoever. She didn't sound genuine or honest. I prepared the food, and continued to serve and clean. The next day I went back to clean the whole house, and waited for all to return after the funeral. When they did, Dawn whom I didn't believe, who had cried so hard on my shoulder, came to me and said that I wasn't needed any longer, and it was time for me to get out of her mother's house. I asked how am I to get home, since I lived fifteen miles away. She said, "You know where the phone is." My husband, Paul came later to get me, I cried hard, not for myself, but for Sharon and Dawn, who had told me to get out of the church. It was so wrong, maybe it was my fault since I didn't stand up for myself.

I think by this time my question: "What must we do to be a good Christian?" was finally answered for me. We all come from our mother's womb, and we are all God's Children. It doesn't matter what we do, as long as we do what is right from our hearts, because that is where God really is. God doesn't judge us for being rich or poor, or pretty or ugly, or for what we have or don't have. We come here naked, with the loan of a human form for a short time. For all material things will be left behind, including our human forms. I think it's what we do for others when they are in need, without giving a thought of who they are, what they have, or what they have done. It is not our right to judge another, but to spread our wings to give all we can of ourselves to the very people who desecrate us. We each have to answer for our own actions, and as long as we love one another and let God stay in our hearts, I will always believe we all shall enter God's Kingdom as his Children! Jesus Christ stood with me through many hardships of my life, so that I could be: "The Ultimate Survivor!"

Horses!

About the age of one-and-a-half, I sat on my first horse. After that nice ride, I'd had my run with them. Then, when I was about sixteen, my step-dad's aunt Libby and uncle John lived on Sand Mountain on a farm. Well, I begged Uncle John for the two weeks I was there to let me ride his horse. Then my parents came up on Saturday, he said ok, I could ride. My step-dad said it was okay. Well, he brought the horse out and saddled her up. They helped me up on her, because she was huge! He showed me how to use the reins and get her to turn around when we reached the end of the long dirt road. Great! I'm a cowgirl! It felt good sitting on Star, but she was walking too slow. She wouldn't giddy-up for me. As we reached the end of the road, she turned around with a G-ha and willingly walked back to the farm. Suddenly a noise came from the bushes on my left. It was my little brother with his bike. That really spooked Star! Oh, great! Now I could be a cowgirl! Yippee! She was running so fast that I lost the reins and had to grab her mane! The saddle went under her belly; I was flopping up and down in the air on her back! My step-dad and Uncle John ran in front of her to stop her. She reared up and bucked me off; I went sailing through the air! I landed at the base of a tree in a ditch on my back, afraid to even move. I heard everyone screaming. My eyes opened, and there was the horse flying over me! My mother and aunt Libby came out screaming at the top of their lungs. I couldn't move. It felt like my back was broken. My step-dad and his aunt helped me up and told me to walk. I tried; whew, that hurt, and they began laughing really loud. When I hit the ditch, it was so hard that my shorts, underwear and all, were split!!!! How lucky could I get to come out with only a sore back and bruises? The poor horse had jumped the gate and damaged her front leg.

That night at dinner I listened while everyone was caught up in their version of what they saw. Mother said, as they were fixing dinner, she glanced out the window just in time to see me sailing through the air. They laughed and were having a good time over the situation. All I could think about was how much I loved horses, and knew the rule. If you fall off, get right back on or you'll never ride again. Everyone was so caught up in their stories that they never noticed I had left the room. The closer I got to Star, the more I talked to her, I knew what I must do. Suddenly, she reared up at me hitting the gate. She wouldn't let me get near her. Walking away with tears in my eyes, I went in the barn and cried like a baby. But I never got to ride her again. Later that night Uncle John told us that Star had not been ridden in nearly five years!

When I was 21, my husband, Paul bought a horse, a solid black beauty, and 15 hands high! My husband knew of my experience with Star. It took 6 months before I felt confident enough to ride on the beauty he had bought. One Sunday, brave me got up on the horse since my husband insisted, it seemed easy enough. About four steps later, the black took off with me in a wild sprint! I pulled the reins, but he had no intention of stopping. Just as we got to the street, my husband's sister, Annie pulled up right in front of the horse with her car, and the horse halted to a dead stop. I told her husband, Ben to grab the reins fast! The horse, turning, was ready to bolt again! Ben helped me off, and that was the last time I ever sat on a horse! I still love them so much. but that wasn't my last wild meeting with a horse.

We had moved to the country, where I had met Donna that owned chicken houses and a number of horses, plus she took in foster kids. She loved riding and was nearly 6 feet tall. One day, while they were checking the new chicks, I had found her newborn colt. A beauty he was. My camera in hand, I took some pictures, and then called Donna and Paul to come down to see the newborn. She had not seen it, and wasn't too happy about me finding it; she didn't even know it had been born. The little thing stood there as we rubbed our scents on him, so he would be used to humans.

Donna and Paul stood there talking about the horses, and as I stepped back to take more photos, I wanted to share them with her. I looked at them with my eyes big, and asked what in the world was that? Out of nowhere, we heard the loudest thunder of hoofs! Sounded just like a stampede, we all three looked at the same time. The papa horse was racing for me as if he could kill me! Paul and Donna ran to get between us! She caught him by the mane as he tried to get past her. They told me to run and get behind the big oak tree. I did! But the horse was still trying to get at me. Donna screamed out that she couldn't hold him much longer, and for me to run like hell and get out of the pasture to the other side of the fence! My husband said later that she popped the horse a big one with her fist, and it calmed him down enough for her to let him go. I heard the thunder again! I looked back and the big horse was in a full run for me! I was almost to the gate! But my heart was beating so hard, I was afraid he would go jump the fence. I didn't take time to open the gate, just jumped it! Looking back, I saw the horse was running fast enough for me to believe he would jump also. Still running, I grabbed the barn door and jumped inside to get out of his sight! Later, Donna said he had never attacked like that before, and that it wasn't his first-born. He had been curious before, but had never attacked anyone like he did me. My husband said, "Don't blame the horse; it's not him, it's her," pointing his finger at me.

I'd never been afraid of horses, even after I was thrown. No one knew what caused the horses to not like me. For the rest of my life, the horses I met let me photograph them, hug them, scratch them, and talk to them. But if I walked to the side of them as if to ride, they changed and acted wild. Maybe they sensed something about me.

U.F.O.?

On a Friday night in October, we came home from shopping with our groceries. It was a big deal since we lived so far from the grocery store. But for the last 6 weeks I had seen an orange light on the mountain where we were still living in the country. One day Paul and I adventured a hike up the mountain in the direction from which the light came. We got half way up the mountain and he whispered, "Go back, go back!" Confused I shook my head and asked why? He pushed my shoulder saying go! Running from what, I had no idea. Finally at the bottom, I stopped and asked him what were we running from? He told me not to ever go up there. I asked why again. He said he didn't know if someone had a whiskey steel up there or what, but when he looked toward the top of the mountain, he didn't know what he saw or what happened, but the hair on his neck stood straight up and a weird feeling came over him to run. He had never felt anything like it before. He never would talk about it again,

When Paul and the girls saw the light, they would chime in saying, "Hey mom, there's your light again." That night we were taking the groceries from the car; the light looked different. It felt as if it was drawing me to it. I went to the middle of the highway and walked a few hundred feet. I felt really light on my feet. Blink, the light went out, I looked to the sky that was dark with bright stars. There were so many like sugar crystals on black velvet. No light on the mountain, but I couldn't move to return back to the house.

A huge object hovered over me, pulling me to it. Where is my family? Why don't they come back to the car? I looked at this huge thing and all I could see was the outer shape of it blocking the stars. I felt so light, as if I was being lifted from the ground. I thought of my daughters. I spoke aloud calmly, "I can't go with you now. I can't leave my daughters; they are so young. Maybe I can meet you here in ten years." It let go of me, and disappeared to my left. The stars were above me again. Walking back to the car, I asked myself what had just happened? Memories flooded my head of hearing about this happening to others, except they were taken. Why didn't they just say they could not go at that time? Taking an armload of groceries from the car, I went into the house. Oh God! What am I seeing??? What has happened? What is going on? I sucked in my breath and stared, afraid to even move.

Paul, Casey, and Sonja, stood perfectly still, as if they were frozen in the middle of their conversation. I could see popcorn in Casey's mouth, the whole kernel, and her boyfriend, Grant, stood next to her. I know what I saw! The grocery bags were still in their hands in mid-air. At that moment, I stared and wondered what would have happened to them if I had not refused. Would they have died standing there? Would they have continued to live and look for me? Why I spoke to them, I'll never know. My mouth opened and I said, "What . . . ?????" They all four started talking at the same time, I just stared at them. My husband looked at his watch, then at me. He knew something had happened, with the lapsed time. Looking at his watch for the second time, he asked where I had been. Why did it take me so long to come from the car? I kept quiet about what I saw, but I did tell them the light was gone. I watched for two years, and it never came again. Some time later the next year we moved to the bottom of the same mountain where the light use to be. I would walk back to the old house to look for the light, it never returned. One day, alone and bored, I decided to hike the mountain to the top. Coming to a rock wall, I decided to climb it instead of going around. Reaching the top, it seems odd that it was completely flat. I knew the light was to my left direction, after walking a piece it seemed like I was pushing against plastic and could go no further. Walking back and forth I tried to go a little further, I couldn't. So I continued off to the right on the top. Strange that is continued to be a flat wooded surface where it should be in peaks. Finally giving up after hearing a low roaring sound, I tracked back down the mountain.

Years after we had moved back to our home town, I drove back to where the old house use to be, it had long since burned down. Standing there waiting for dark, I wondered if anyone else had ever seen the same bright orange light, or to afraid to speak in fear of being thought crazy. It was getting late so I guess the light was gone from the mountain forever. On my way home my thoughts wondered, I'll never know what would have happened if I had went with them. I as others thought folks made up what they saw, but a little of myself wondered why would they make up such, plus there were so many folks around the world that had seen the same thing I did. There is something out there.

Will anyone ever believe me?

The Last Beating

Paul and I had moved back to our hometown. We not only left the country, but our daughters Casey and Sonja also. They had chosen to get married and live with their husbands in the country. We didn't like the new area that we moved to, but we had the chance to buy a house. It had two bedrooms, so one was made into a guest room, just in case the girls decided to visit for a night or two. I thought to myself, things are finally going right since the doctor told me I only had a year left to live. He said my body was totally worn out. I did not want to die in the country alone. What I didn't know is that depression can actually make you want to die.

About three months later, Paul came home and told me our youngest, Sonja, had called him at work. It seems that her husband had been married before and owed child support, which he never paid. So he was put in jail. Sonja had begged her dad to co-sign with her for the money, so she could get her husband out of jail. I begged my husband not to; let him clear his own mistakes, he will never learn anything if you make it easy for him. But he went with her to the bank and signed papers. When he came home, I told him that it was a big mistake to do that. He said he did it to keep her family from moving back home with us. I said, "It won't work! That's not the way life is."

Things seemed to be going so well, and we were able to start saving. I knew it felt too good for the first time in years for some reason. What a beautiful day, I was singing and cleaning my new home. Oh, there's the postman! Mail came with bills, sale papers, and a letter. When I saw the bank's name on it, my heart almost stopped. Holding my breath, I opened it. Sonja's husband was late with the first payment. Paul called them, Sonja said, "It's ok, Dad, we can pay it Friday." I looked at my husband, then he said, "Don't say it." I didn't.

The house seemed to be coming together pretty good. As the days passed I made progress with the improvements. Another month went by, and we managed to buy a camper. We camped in the same mountains for 21 years. It was nice to not be caught out in the rain with a tent, especially when a tornado passed through. Of course the girls and their families came to barbecue. Everyone was so happy, even our first baby grandson. But as I was watching all of them, a little mean thought tiptoed into my mind. "There's too much happiness; what's going on? What do they know that we don't?" It's like the quiet before the storm.

All went well as we were on our way home, I told Paul everyone was too happy. There's something going on. He knew my intuitions were 99% right. I think he felt it also, but he never said anything until Monday when the mail came. Of course the bank sent us a terrible letter stating they would take our land, house, and camper, and anything else of value, if we didn't pay off the bank note that Paul had co-signed with Sonja. There had been only one payment made in three months. Everything inside of me fell to the floor, for the first time in many years, we finally had a small savings. Paul and I had to collect every cent we had, even our pennies in a jar, to pay off the loan he had co-signed on. My heart totally broke into pieces, but finding strength in my willpower, I knew that we could start again.

Staying busy was no problem, with the house and yard. But, without money, we couldn't go far with any improvements. So we waited. Then one day our oldest daughter, Casey, showed up at the door with her son Jamie, and all of her baggage. She and her husband had split. Another month later Sonja was standing at the door with her son Chris and all of their belongings. What was I going to do? The guest bedroom contained four guests, split the room is my only solution.

My daily routine started from early morning until late at night to keep the housework under control. The laundry never ended; also the same with dish washing. There was no way anyone could convince me that my daughters were so lazy, changing their babies' clothing three or four times a day and arguing. Even my husband started leaving early for work. I had no place to go, just had to stay home, at times go behind the garden shed and cry like a baby.

At the beginning of hunting season, we took the camper up to the mountain and left it in a hunter's camp. There it could sit until hunting season was over. Then Thanksgiving came with the massive cooking. I thought, well I wouldn't invite anyone, since we had so little with six to feed. We ended up with many guests anyway. Casey and Sonja were especially rude that night after everyone left. With my feelings being hurt so much, my eyes never saw many dry days anymore. Paul grabbed my hand for me to follow him to the bedroom, and he asked, "Why don't we go to the camper? Let them have the house." As we were leaving, a thought came to me as I saw my daughters laughing while watching us load the truck. I told Paul, "They just ran us out of our own home." He stopped as he was backing out of the driveway, saying: "I can't believe that just happened." Back into the house he went. I could hear yelling, but not what they were saying. Then we left as he said, "Don't worry; things will be different when we come back. I won't put up with them like you do." I just kept quiet with my thoughts, he won't put up with them? He's the one that hit the road all of the time and left me behind, so when had he ever put up with them?

We came back on Sunday night to find Casey and Jamie gone with her new boyfriend. She had met him at her job, which didn't last long. Later I found out they had a fight in our bedroom and broke some of my keepsakes, what were they doing in our bedroom? This was the beginning of what was to come in the next year. Paul had changed again, leaving and not saying where he was going or when he'd be back. He and our daughters were coming and going, as if they lived in a hotel with free housekeeping service. If I said anything, they said I was a horrible person. So I cried out behind the buildings and continued serving them, with the hopes they would go to work or get remarried. I couldn't cast them out; maybe I should have. I was my mother's slave, did all I was told, and she still tossed me out. There was one difference: I loved my family very much.

During this time I learned how to preserve and can vegetables and fruit. One day I realized that I had been home for more than six weeks, cleaning, cooking, and working in the garden. I asked my husband to please take me somewhere, even for a ride. I just needed to get out of the house for a little while. He said, "Sure, right after dinner." While the five of them ate, I showered, fixed my hair, and even put on a little makeup. As they finished eating, I wrapped the leftovers and stored them in the fridge. The kitchen was clean to perfection. I was humming softly with my thought of going away from the house. Paul was talking to our Sonja, and I asked if he was ready to go. Oh yes, he was. As I walked to the truck, he said, "Hey, I want to talk to dad a minute." A little pain of disappointment came to me, I asked if we would leave soon. "Oh yes," he said. Why were these sick feelings coming in my stomach? Why? He held my hand walking to his mother's, just two houses away. I went into the kitchen with her. As she made coffee, she was asking me why I was fixed up so pretty. I told her of our plans. She replied, "Well, that's good; you need to get out for awhile. You've been home just too much."

We could hear Paul, his two brothers, and dad yelling over the wrestling show on the television. Finishing the cup of coffee, I asked Paul if he was ready to go. He screeched at me, "When I'm good and ready!" I heard them laughing at his comment of authority as I went back to the kitchen. I waited until he called saying in a hateful tone, "If you want to go, then come on!" As we walked up the street, I asked him why he spoke to me that way in front of his family. I accepted his apology, and then I asked if he would wait a minute, because I had to go to the bathroom. He said sure, no problem. As I walked in, Sonja had the TV on cartoons for her son, another thing I had had to give up: TV. Then I saw my kitchen, with food from the fridge on the table among dirty dishes and glasses. It was clean just thirty minutes ago! I asked Sonja who had made the mess. She said Casey's boyfriend was hungry so they all ate again, and she didn't want clean it up. I just shook my head. When I came from the bathroom, there sat Paul watching wrestling with Sonja and Chris, she hated wrestling and I knew it. I asked Paul did he see the kitchen? "Yeah, I did," he replied. I told him I was ready to go if he was. He screeched, "NO, not till you clean the kitchen!" My heart sank to the pit of my stomach. "Please," I begged; I'll do it when we get back." He screamed, "NO!" Staring at him the pressure on my chest felt as if a time bomb was going to explode. Sonja looked at me with a smirky smile, as if to say, "I told you I wouldn't do it." As I walked to the door, Paul stopped me, saying that I had better clean that table off, "NOW!" I explained that I had just cleaned it thirty minutes before. He said that he didn't care, that it was my duty to clean it up again! So many things were flying through my mind: the laundry, cooking, dishes, my daughter's disrespect, my grandsons arguing and messing up many things. My daughters letting their sons sling popsicle juice on my new Pricilla curtains, or giving them a bottle showing them how to squirt milk or juice on the furniture. Some of the keepsakes I'd had since my childhood, and would be passed on to them one day. My mother taught me to never break or destroy anything. But I couldn't deal with this anymore! As Paul turned to see what I was doing, staring at him, I asked calmly, "You want that table cleaned off?" He demanded that if I wanted to go for a ride, then I had better get it done. Thoughts flooded my mind: "He has no intention of taking me anywhere; if so, it would be to the river to watch others fishing or what ever he wanted." Walking to the table, I saw my mother's antique bowls sitting there with remaining scraps of food from the second go around of dinner. Looking back at my husband, I asked, "Are you sure we'll go riding if I clean the table off?" He nodded his head saying, yeah, yeah, yeah, while watching the television.

That's when the bomb exploded in my chest. All of my strength that I thought had drained out of me came to life as I picked up the end of the table and flipped it. Dishes, glasses, bowls, silverware, food, all were flying. Twirling around with a smile and dusting my hands, I simply said, "Ok, the table is clean; can we leave now?" My daughter's mouth flew wide open. She had never seen me do anything like this before, nor had I. Paul looked at me, screaming, "YOU STUPID BITCH! CLEAN IT UP!" Still smiling, I walked to the doorway of the living/dining room. I asked again very calmly, "Are you going to take me for a ride?" He snarled and told me how stupid he thought I was and I had better clean it up!

Above the stove was a double shelf where my precious four pieces of crystal tiers were sitting, with a set of punch cups hanging on the out edge around the top shelf. He was mumbling to Sonja how crazy and stupid I was. Another bomb went off through my fist as it hit the first piece of crystal, shattering it into a thousand pieces. Hitting the second one, Paul screamed at me, saying, "If you know what's good for you, you'll get busy cleaning up the mess you've made! Hit one more thing, just one more, and I'll fix you!" I looked at him and said, "All I destroyed is mine, and you never say anything about what the kids do. When you get angry with them or your family, you beat on me." He just said, "Go ahead, and break one more thing."

My fist flew out to the first cup that was hanging before me. I didn't care if it cut me or not. I hit it with all of the force in my fist! He jumped up, grabbed me by the yoke of my shirt, and started pounding my face. He hit me so hard he couldn't hold on to me, and backwards I flew after the third punch. Our big microwave was sitting on a stand three feet behind me; as I flew back, my head hit the sharp corner. I felt the pain as I fell to the floor, unconscious. The fall caused me to wake up; slowly I stood up. Three times he knocked me into the microwave; three times he knocked me out. The last time in the floor, I felt the back of my head with my hand, and there was so much blood. Anger flew through my whole body. As I tried to get up, he said, "Please, babe, don't get up again; I don't want to hit you anymore. Stay down." My face was hurting, with my head bleeding; I tasted blood in my mouth. All I could see was Sonja laughing behind Paul, with him standing there with his fist ready for me again. I can still see her face today; I think that hurt more than the punches he gave me. I told her not to laugh, that at the rate she was going, her payday would come sooner than she knew. As I walked towards her, he grabbed me and gave one hard punch to my face. I flew backwards from the living room to the kitchen floor. I could take no more. All of my strength had left me to stand-alone. I made my way to the bed, and sleep came so easily. Why did I not call the police? What good would it do? If I filed charges against him, he would be out the next morning and do it again only worse. All of the beatings he gave me put so much fear into me of what was to come next. But you know, he never noticed that the cup I hit flipped up in the air and sat straight up on the dining room table.

To look back now, I remember the shame I felt about my appearance when he finished with me after each beating. I swore to myself this would be his last time, after I looked into the mirror the next morning. There were slits for eyes. If I had not known who I was, there was no way I could have recognized myself. As I went for coffee, they were cleaning up the mess. Without a scratch on him, he only said once that he was sorry, but also said it was my fault he had to do this to me for twenty-eight years.

Even after two days, I still couldn't open my eyes, my face still doubled in size. He had taken my mother and stepfather's word to beat me at least once a week, whether I needed it or not, to keep me in line to serve him. It just wasn't as often as they wanted.

The third day there wasn't as much pain, and the holes on the back of my head seemed to be healing. My headaches had subsided to minor. I had just finished the dinner dishes, when I saw Paul's parents walking up the hill to our house. I ran into the living room, shaking, asking him not to let them come in. He told me to behave. I ran to the bathroom, but as he let them in, he told me to make some coffee, because his mother and daddy were there. What choice did I have but to do as told? I turned my head away from them, as his dad sat down in front of the television. His mom came into the kitchen. I asked her if she would like some coffee, she said that would be nice. As I finished I kept washing the counter so she couldn't see my face. Then she said my name three times, Marion, I asked, what? Marion, Marion? I thought, "Okay, if you want to see what your son did to me, fine!" Without a doubt I knew someone had told her. As I turned around, her mouth dropped wide open, and she went as pale as a ghost. I stared straight into her eyes and said: "It's not the first time for me, but it's your first to see what he does to me." She called to her husband and said they had to go! Then she said, "Son, I want you to come to my house, now." They left, not even drinking the coffee I made. He asked me what happened, I shrugged. A few minutes later he followed them. When he came back, he made me get into his truck. I pleaded with him, because I didn't want anyone to see me this way. He made me go anyway. Whatever his mother said worked for nearly a year, even though he made his threats by saying, "Remember the last time!" As the days went by, the fear would come and go in my chest.

Then, almost a year later to that date, he made me stay at the house for three months. One morning his mom called to me outside, wanting me to come down to have coffee. I went in to get my cigarettes and quietly going out the side door, in hopes I wouldn't be seen by Paul. As I got to the end of the driveway, he shouted: "Who said you could leave this yard?" He scared me so bad I messed my shorts all the way back in the house to the bathroom. He laughed at me for weeks, stomping his foot at me as if he would hit me. When he was home, I couldn't even go to the mailbox in front of our house for fear of what might happen. By this time our daughters and grandsons had moved out. Paul started staying home more often since we were alone. I did all I could to stay out of his way.

One Saturday night he told me he would be right back, but I thought he meant he would go to his mom's. He left in the truck, returning with beer and cigarettes. I asked him if we could go riding or something. "NO!!!!! I'm going to watch wrestling!" With that reply, I said no more to him. I hated wrestling with a passion, and he knew it. So I got a couple of magazines to read, a beer, and my cigarettes. I went into the bedroom, closed the door, turned on some country music, and got comfortable. Before I finished the first story, he opened the bedroom door, asking me why I had the door closed; what was I doing? I simply said it was to listen to the radio without hearing wrestling in the background. I asked him to close the door back. He looked at me and said: "Leave the door open!" I agreed to leave it as it was. I gave him a few minutes to get back in front of the TV; then I closed the door very quietly.

I finished my story and started another one. As I was reading, it occurred to me that I lived my life through the lives of others. As I continued reading, I felt fine, almost too good. At that moment the door opened, and he gritted his teeth, saying, "I told you to leave this damn door open if you know what's good for you!" I asked what was his problem for me to have the door closed? "It's my house; now keep it open!" he said. A few minutes later, I almost had the door closed when, BAM! It flew open, knocking me back and making a big hole in the wall. Don't ask me where my fear went, I have no idea. I clenched my fist and asked him what was wrong with him, very loud but not screaming. The next thing I knew before I finished my sentence was that he had grabbed me up by the yoke of my shirt, with his fist drawn back to punch me. A flash went through my head like a bolt of lightning. "My kids are gone; I live in a prison with this controlling freak! I know without a doubt, on this night *I am going to die,* but as God is my witness, not without a fight!!! In my heart and mind, I knew he would kill me. I think God gave me the strength to do what I did next. My husband's fist was coming to my face, but before it got to me, I spit right in his face. My voice had changed into what, I don't know, but it came out of my mouth with a deep growling sound, and I knew my teeth were showing. It sounded as if I had turned into a mad, rabid dog. After I spit in his face, the growl spoke, "I can't take this anymore; go ahead and hit me, but you damn well better kill me; cause if you don't, I'll kill you before daylight!!! Do you hear me???? I'll kill you before daylight!!! I can stay awake longer than you! I can out drink you! I can outsmart you! I can do everything better than you, except hurt you as you have me!!!! Go ahead; beat me again! Make it twenty-nine years!!! Go ahead, you stupid son-of-a-bitch!!!!!!!! What are you waiting for???????? Hit me!!!!!!!!! I want to kill you!!!!!"

My teeth were grinding the grit from the broken ones from my bottom teeth. Our eyes were locked. His fist dropped; then he lowered me down to the floor. Something gave in my chest, like a sigh of relief, as I glared at his pale face. Two things were going through my mind: one, he bought it; two, is it over? I should have stood up to him years ago, but until this time I thought this was the way of life. I could never hit or hurt anyone like I have been, but enough is enough. My punishment from him was far from being over, but he never hit me again!

Dedicated to My Sister and Mother

Sunday, while I was preparing dinner, the phone rang. It was Casey, saying she was coming for a visit and bringing Lacy with her. I said okay, but asked why she was bringing my sister here. "Mom, Lacy is staying with me, and she wants to tell you something," my daughter replied. Letting out a sigh, I said, "Okay, come and eat dinner with us. I'll have plenty prepared, then wondered what Lacy was up to now, for in the past she had told so many lies and hurt my feelings beyond repair. We were half-sisters, and I never heard the end of it. Our last meeting was three years before, with not a very happy parting. They came just before I had dinner ready. Lacy sat at the kitchen table and said to me, "Marion, if you die before me, I'll always remember you standing in front of a stove. You've always cooked for us when we came to visit." I thought, "What a strange thing for her to say." Looking at her, I asked if that was what she had come to tell me. Replying no, she said, "I've come to tell you that I am dying." She was lighting a cigarette, and I asked her to go outside to smoke. Casey looked at me with a frown and said, "Mom, she is dying!" "Sorry, but she has to go out; you know I don't smoke anymore Casey." They went outside for a while.

"Food's ready; come and get it while it's hot," I called. Looking at my sister, I wondered if this was her way to get back into my heart. Was she lying again? I questioned her on what the doctors had said. With her answers, I was still in doubt. Time would tell, since she had less than a year to live. With so many doubts, and the reminder of the heartaches of the past, it was hard to see ahead. Was she telling the truth?

Time passed with summer and the holidays, then winter, and the New Year. I hadn't seen Lacy since the last Easter, but had heard that she had an apartment about 50 miles away, and was on disability. Then in the second week of January, she called asking me to come for a visit. On my arrival, I noticed she had visitors, and she all but ignored me. The question was, "Why did you call and ask me to come?" She only replied that she wanted to see me, but she was going out and that I had come at a bad time to visit. In the meantime she was getting ready to go out to a nightclub with her friends. Staring at her, I had to say, "So, you just wanted to see if I'd jump and run when you beckoned me, again! You are so much like our mother." Leaving, with my feelings so hurt, I promised myself that I'd never run to her again. The last of January passed, with February behind. The days began to warm up, and with the spring housecleaning finished, I decided to visit my only old aunt Matilda. While I was sitting with her eating lunch, the phone rang. It was Paul calling to say Lacy had taken a turn for the worst, and she wouldn't live much longer. Immediately I asked, "Is it another summons, a joke, or what?" He believed it was the real thing this time. I told him I'd go and check it out. I told aunt Matilda what it was about, and left to go to my sister's home.

Spending a few hours there, I saw my sister in bed, not able to get up. Her hands were curled, with a long emery board between her fingers, and an alphabet board in front of her. She couldn't speak anymore, so she picked the letters out to communicate with others. Several people were there from the family that had abandoned me, my step dad, his new wife, my half brother with his wife and her two daughters. Looking around, no one was cooking, cleaning, or anything, just complaining of no sleep. That day was Tuesday, and someone needed to take control of the situation. I told Lacy, her daughter, and Casey that I would be back the next morning, prepared to help. They seemed grateful to know that I was coming back. On my way home, I planned what to cook for Paul to last a few days. When he came home I told him the situation, and that I was going to stay with Lacy until the end. He only said not to worry; he would be okay. How sympathetic he was for her, why not, he used to date her while I was at work. The next morning, with my clothes packed, I left for the bank to get a little cash. When I arrived, nothing had been moved, only added: dirty dishes everywhere, clothes scattered, and a real bad stench. I said hello to all and got busy. After two hours of cleaning the kitchen, I felt compelled to cook. Not one thing to fix. I told them if they got some food that I'd cook for them. One neighbor and my step-dad took me to the store, and they decided they wanted homemade spaghetti. Okay by me. After awhile, all of them were eating, so I decided to sit with Lacy and talk to her. She used the alphabet board to answer or ask me questions. Repeatedly, she asked for her other two sisters, Lynn and Sophie. (I was the half-sister to the four siblings. She was a twin, five years younger than me; there was a brother four years younger than her; and the baby girl, fifteen years younger than me.) I did all I could to get them to come. My half-brother, his wife, my step dad, and his new wife were all there. My daughter, with my sister's daughter, took care of her when she became bedridden.

    Wednesday night all the others left to go home, saying they would come back in the morning. I felt as if I should sit with her. I noticed she was staring so hard at me. I told her I could only imagine what she was thinking. She asked what I thought she had on her mind. So I looked her straight in the eyes and said, "I know you don't want me here, do you?" With the emery board in her hand she let me know the answer was, "NO!"

I looked at her and said, "Sorry, but you are stuck with me! You don't see the rest of your family here, do you? You've spent your life doing for your sisters and brother, but look who is here with you." There was a faint smile in her eyes; I think to let me know it was okay. It was just too quiet for me. My mouth opened, saying, "Hey, when you get to heaven would you dig a little hole and pull me through?" Her eyes lit up, and I swear you could see her smile. I think she knew then that I believed her. It got quiet again, and my thoughts of Mother came to me. I told Lacy that after Mother died, she came to me, and not understanding it scared me. So I asked her if she was going to come back and let me know she made it just fine. She let me know she would by blinking her eyes once for yes and twice for no. She blinked once. I asked, "You promise?" Once again she blinked, only once. I told her I wouldn't be scared this time. At this point, she couldn't hold the emery board because her body was getting hard fast.

After our daughters would feed her through the tube in her stomach, she would sleep. They tiptoed out quietly, but we could hear voices in her room. No television was on, and Lacy couldn't speak, but her voice was heard. Later, her daughter questioned her; she had seen Mother, OUR Mother, who died in 1978. I told them it could be possible, since death is still a sequence of the human after life that even scientists don't understand.

We slept here and there that night. I woke up with the need for the bathroom very early. As I finished, and washed my hands, strange noises and shouting were coming from Lacy's room. With the towel still in my hand, I walked into the room, hearing my niece saying loudly, "WALK INTO THE LIGHT, MAMMA" repeatedly. I looked and my daughter Casey stood facing the corner of the room; my niece was facing the window. I asked what was going on. Lacy was gasping for her breath. God help me, she was so scared! I pulled the cot up to her bed and sat, with her hard, cold hands in mine. Looking her straight in the eyes, I said, "You are scared, aren't you?" She blinked once. I said, "Okay, but listen to me. I promise you there is nothing to be afraid of. Remember how much Mother loved you; with all of my heart I know she and Jesus are very close. They're waiting for you; they won't leave without you. They love you too much, Lacy. Just relax; it's very easy, I promise, no more pain. She fixed her eyes on mine, and then suddenly the life separated from her body, with no more pain and no more fear, just peace.

Our daughters still had their backs turned. I told them, "It's okay now; she's gone." Then my niece said, "Oh my God, here comes Granddaddy; it will kill him!" I said, "Don't worry about him! My God, your mother just died; take care of her! I'll take care of your granddaddy." I asked my niece what was to be done next, and she replied that she had to call the home nurse. I said, "Go call now." Without hesitating, she did. I went to the hall and stopped Lacy's father (my step dad). Looking him in the eyes, I told him she was gone. For the first time since I was a child, he grabbed me, hugging me because of his loss. I whispered, "I know you would rather see me lying there instead of your favorite daughter." After what he had contributed to my life, I felt no sympathy for him. They didn't want to look at her, so I went back into the room and waited for the nurse. I didn't even know when she entered the room, but as I turned, she took the hose from Lacy's stomach. All I saw was oozing green, and the nurse said, "Oh my God, I'm so sorry!" Somebody grabbed me, and out of the room we went. The strength came back to my legs as I looked around the room, and no one even saw me when I picked up my bag and walked out, feeling numb. When I got into the truck, I had to sit a minute. I felt as if my job was over. No one said I'm sorry for your loss, or goodbye, nothing.

It was more than 30 miles that I drove before it hit me. "She's gone, my sister is gone!" Shaking, crying, I was trying to drive. When I pulled out onto the highway, everything was so blurred that I had to pull the truck to the side. I was crying so hard that I didn't see or hear the highway patrolman who was at my truck window. He knocked, and I looked up, and then opened the window a little. He asked if there was a problem. I told him my sister had died about 30 minutes before, and it just now hit me. I pulled over because I couldn't see to drive. He said I did the right thing, and asked if he could call someone for me. I looked at him, thinking about the people that I used to call my family. I shook my head, saying, "No, there's no one for me." He told me to stay there until I felt better. After I gained control, I noticed an unmarked police car sitting across the highway, waiting patiently for me.

When I finally got home, my husband was leaving to go to work. He asked if I wanted him to stay home, and I saw no reason for him to do that. He told me to go out to eat and not just sit there. So I did, but when I returned home, there was a sweet smell of cologne in front of my stove. I knew that scent; several times I walked back and forth sniffing the air. It dawned on me later that it was the cologne Lacy wore: White Shoulders. She had died early that morning. I tried to forget the scent that was connected to her in hopes that someone had been there in my absence. When I asked my husband about it, I told him it was very important to let me know. He said no, that he'd been the only one there. The next day I left the house to buy a dark suit to wear to the funeral. On returning, I came in the same way as always. When I reached the area where my stove stood, there was a strong odor. I had to think real hard to remember what it was: formaldehyde! I remembered the smell of it when Mother passed. My heart raced when I thought of what Lacy and I had talked about a few days before.

All my life I've believed in three's, and I know my sister knew of this. The next day I left without thinking of the strange odors. But when I got home, the same spot in front of my stove had a strong sweet odor of Swisher Sweet cigar. Only Lacy and I would be the ones to remember the time she and I smoked her husband's cigars from the dash of his car. I faced the wall, my heart pounding in my chest so hard that I didn't know what to do. "It is true! The dead can contact the living!" I spoke aloud, saying,

"Okay, Lacy, I know it's you letting me know you made it just fine; now go and rest in peace!" My heart would not slow down. So I took long, deep breaths and tried to relax. Waiting, I wondered, "If I tell anyone, will they believe me?" Lacy died three days before Mother's birthday; then buried on that very day: March 31st, 1995. Paul would not even look at her after she died, I still wonder why?

Final Years

The next couple of years were better than usual after the last beating, even though he threatened me a year later. Knowing he had been with another woman, I just told him to go ahead. "If you want to hit me, go ahead, but be ready for the consequences." I reminded him of my vows the year before. Still knowing what was going on, I tried to convince myself that it didn't matter. I was working hard to establish good customer relations, to build up my clientele for my wedding cake and painting sales.

Each time he would come in and yell at me, I wondered where he was going so early before work and coming in so late at night. On my way to work one day, I saw his jeep sitting at a hamburger place. I stopped to see him, and wondered why he was there. I had prepared a cooked meal for his lunch. He never acknowledged my presence, even when I touched him. He shoved my arm to the side, looking at her as he walked past me to go out the door. If I could just make myself turn around, I could see the woman he was with sitting on my left. For some reason, I couldn't look. It was if it would be the final straw to end my marriage. Of course, later, Paul denied everything. He never saw me.

Nearly a year later, he used my truck to drive and I drove his jeep to work, he wanted to go up on a mountain to get two maple trees we had marked the fall before. I didn't think anything about it until the following

Monday, when Paul took his jeep leaving me the truck. I put my lunch and purse in the front seat, it was obvious that a woman had been sitting on the passenger side and had emptied the cuff of her jeans on the floor. I could still see her footprints. God? Would this ever end? Why is he like this?

Sonja was living at the house on the opposite corner from us, so I called her. I asked her to watch and see what time her dad came in from work. She asked me some questions and started crying, saying, "Oh, Mom, I never believed you! Then she told me her story. Now what am I going to do? Call work, and tell them an emergency came up." I left the house and parked where no one could see me. I waited for him to arrive home, and then drove to the house. As I walked in calmly, Paul looked strange, asking why am I at home? I told him we needed to talk. He said, "Okay, what's up?" I stood before him on the opposite side of the table, so if he tried to hit me, I could have one way or another to run. Then I told him to sit down and listen. He did, and I asked, "Paul, is there something you want to tell me?" He said, "No." I told him I was giving him every chance to come clean. He just stared at me with his fist doubled up. I could feel the pain as I stared at his white knuckles. Then I told him that I had spoken with someone on the phone that saw him with another woman. He said it was just somebody trying to start trouble between us, like they did before. Then I stared, asking, "What? What did you just say?" He repeated himself. He went on making excuses and telling me there was no one. When I asked him about the floor in the truck. Now he didn't know how that got there, that I must have made that mess. I explained that I had just cleaned the truck the day before he used it. I knew he wouldn't tell the truth, so I said, "Okay, let's go back to the phone call. Come on; tell me the truth," I screamed! He tried to hug me. Backing off, I knew better than to let him get a grip on me. I backed away, and gave him one last chance to come clean. He wouldn't. So I dialed a number, "Hey, he's here; I need you to hear what he's got to say before you speak to him." He took the phone, cursed, and ranted on about what a liar the person was. He heard someone crying and asked, "Who the hell is this?" The voice on the phone said, "Daddy, it's me, Sonja! I saw you, Daddy! I saw you with that woman in mom's truck!" His face went as white as a sheet. He leaned against the counter, saying, "Oh, my God." Then he went on to tell her what had happened. He hung the phone up and told me, his wife, a story. Our older daughter Casey called, and he told her a story. Three stories in forty minutes, and not one of them was the same. Ready to run, I stared at him. "You are so full of it. You think any of us believed your stories?" I asked. He reared up screaming, "It's the truth!" Shaking my head, I asked, "How could you? We all know you are lying. But you know what? It doesn't matter anymore. You are building your kingdom of hell, and no one will care." I just couldn't understand how he could live with himself, how? I let it all go, and the tears flowed, helping to wash away my pain. Would this ever be over with? How much more could I deal with?

Not long after he started sitting at the door of my job. The management called me in and said he had to go, because he couldn't be sitting there. A couple of weeks later, they let me go, and said when I got my personal life straightened out that I could come back. In my heart I knew it would never be over with. So true, why did I keep trying?

Paul seemed all too happy that I lost my job. I took care of things around the house, making the wedding cakes and landscaping the yard, among other things. Then all of a sudden he was in a big hurry to go quad riding. He knew I had a wedding cake to deliver and set up for three hundred people. After I finished, I drove to where he was supposed to be riding, stopping once to get him a few beers. Just as I started off, he pulled up. I got out and told him I brought him some beer. He made accusations to me, saying he knew better, but he kept looking behind him. A car stopped on the other side of the gas pumps, and a tall young blonde girl got out. The two of them had their eyes locked. I said, "HEY," and asked him if he wanted me to ask the girl what she was looking at. He told me to get in the car and go home, that it was none of my business. The girl was younger than our own daughters. When I looked at the quad runner; two people had been riding it. You could still see the outline where they had been sitting on the seat. Another chunk of my heart fell as I remembered the last time I rode with him. It wasn't pleasant, because he did all he could to sling me off. Finally succeeding, he flew through a creek, knowing I couldn't swim. I tried to hold on to him. It was impossible, and off I went in the middle of the creek, choking and trying to call him for help. He sat there on the quad, laughing at me struggling to get out. Crying, I asked him why he did me that way. Was his girlfriend that important to him? On the fishing boat, he had tried many times to knock me off. He had also crashed me into tree limbs, trying to make me lose my balance so I would fall in the lake. Now that I look back, maybe his intentions were to kill me then. I thought about it for a long time at all the things he did to me.

At the next gathering with my family, we all had fun and a good time. At the end of the gathering, I called Paul, Casey and Sonja together. I announced to them, "I'm warning all three of you. If some changes are not made, within seven years I'll be gone." I told them it was totally up to them. They just laughed, and said, "Oh, you're not going anywhere." I told them to watch, knowing they didn't care. Paul took me in his arms, squeezing me so tight I couldn't breathe, saying: "I'll see you dead before I'll let you go!" I was afraid of him right then! I laughed, and said nervously, "Oh, you know I'm not going anyplace; anyway, where would I go?" He finally let me go, saying, "You heard what I said!" A strong sense of fear had my heart racing. I hoped with time he would forget what I had said, but later, I found out he had not forgotten. After causing me to lose two more jobs, he had me right where he wanted me, at home. I devoted my time to baby-sitting the grandbabies, while still remodelling our house. Landscaping my yard to turn it into a paradise garden. Plus I grew vegetables to can and made jellies from the fruit trees. Wintertime I made quilts, and afghans.

Looking at my family, they seemed to keep going in other directions. Sonja had found out that her husband had a pregnant girlfriend; that was after he had made my daughter abort her own pregnancy. The more I listened to her, the more I heard a breakdown coming. An idea came to me. She needed to know there were more fish in the sea that were nice. So I asked her if she would like to go to the Gulf for a few days. But we had to figure out how to get away from Paul. I knew it would cause a problem. So we decided to tell him we were leaving later than we really were. As we made plans, Paul asked how many days he needed to take off from work. Sonja told him that if he planned on going, we would not go, it was a mother and daughter time. We left a day early, to make sure we could get away from him.

What a grand time she had. I told her to be free-spirited and happy. That was what this was all about, because I didn't want her to suffer the same situations that I had. I watched her receiving all of the attention of the spectators, staring at how really beautiful she was.

A couple of months later, I took our grandsons, Jamie and Chris to Florida, Paul went also since he knew he didn't have to pay for anything. After we arrived, they changed into their swimsuits while I unpacked our luggage. I told the boys to stay in sight of the motel, they chimed in together with an okay as they ran out to the beach. Paul went behind them and I though he was going to look around from the balcony, but instead he had followed the boys around when they were talking to the girls their own age. Coming to me, they would beg me to make him leave them alone. What is he doing, I asked. Both of them talking at the same time telling me he was scaring the girls away by flirting with them, asking them if they want to go with him. I felt so sick, asking the boys are they sure that's what he's doing. I looked out the bay window and there he was following the girls. I gave Jamie and Chris some money to go walking, away from him, I'll make sure he doesn't follow you. I told them to be polite and ask the girls if they could buy them a coke or something, with them on their way, I called Paul and asked what is wrong with him? What did he think he was doing? Paul, why are you acting like a pervert? He just sniggered and walked down the beach in the opposite direction. He didn't want to be with me, he was drunk, on two beers? That didn't make any sense to me. It scared me to think of what I had just seen.

Later Jamie and Chris came back with smiles on their young faces. It pleased me so to see them happy. They had caught up with the girls, and they had ice cream cones instead of cokes. I asked if they had they seen their papa; no they hadn't and didn't want to. I knew he had over four hundred dollars in his pocket. I finished with the unpacking and made dinner, the boys said they were tired from walking and building sand castles. They stayed in the room while I looked everywhere for Paul, he just wasn't to be found. We ate dinner, and very late that night, Paul came home, staggering around and cussing. We had hopped in the beds and pretended to be asleep. His dinner was in the oven, but he turned on the light, ranting that I had better get up and serve him, if I knew what was good for me! I didn't argue. How could that gorgeous man be like that? That night, I checked his wallet: less than two hundred dollars. I didn't ask, afraid to. Nothing showed up to explain the missing money. The next day, before he started drinking, I suggested he take the boys out on a fishing boat. They took photos when the Captain let each of them drive the big fishing boat. They loved it! I knew then it was right to bring them. Paul wouldn't do anything else with our grandsons, so I took them to a theme park, even rode some of the rides with them. They both laughed at me, after I got wet on the log ride, it was funny. We made it home safe from out trip, parting to go our own ways. Later Casey and Sonja called to ask what were the boys talking about.

Things were gradually growing worse. I didn't say anything about Paul's girlfriends anymore. One way of looking at it was that he left me alone during that time. It had been seven months since he even touched me, after my doctor told me my husband had transmitted a disease to me. I stayed away from him as much as possible; lately it was easy since he stayed gone most of the time. Nothing was sacred to this man, not our marriage, family, love or even life. Searching for clues of why life is going this way, Paul and I had a good sexual relationship, we enjoyed camping, hiking, entertaining, fishing and he wanted me to go hunting with him. I didn't go all the time because I know that a man needs his space.

Then one night, after I had worked all day in the greenhouse, he opened a beer for me, saying, "Here, just for you!" After a few sips, I had to lie down on my bed. I stared at the ceiling. Something wasn't right, why couldn't I move? My mind seemed to drift off. What was happening to me? I thought, maybe if I went to sleep, it would be okay when I woke up. But it wasn't! It felt as if an elephant was sitting on me; I couldn't breathe! I managed to get one eye opened a little. It was Paul raping me! Words wouldn't come out of my mouth. Why? Why couldn't I move him? I could only groan in resistance! I could think the words, "Get off," but no sound would come from my mouth. I was praying to God, begging God to "Please get him off of me! Please don't let this be happening!" I knew Paul had given me something, I knew the only thing I had to drink was a few sips of beer. When he finished, he got off of me. I still couldn't get up, not even move my body. Tears were running down each side of my face going into my ears. What is wrong with me? What is wrong with him?

The next morning, he was up before me and went about his business, as if nothing had happened. Confused, I asked myself if I had dreamed it all. Nothing was said, but the fear started building in my chest. It wasn't a dream; my panties were gone. The pain of dry intercourse hurt. I was sore and not losing my mind. It did happen! What was I going to do? Where could I go? I went to my daughter's for help. I knew without any doubt he had drugged me. It had not been long since he had bragged about drugging me so many times in the past, and I never knew it. Arriving at my daughter's home, tears poured out as I told her what Paul did, she wouldn't believe me. She had company, and I went totally numb, I knew what I must do. Leaving, I told my daughter to forget it, that I was sorry I even bothered her. Jumping in my car, I spun off in the gravel, knowing the territory quite well. Going to the end of the road there was a long, paved road. And at one end, I knew about the tree on the curve. I didn't want to live; I knew how to end it all. Going as far as I dared, I turned the car around. I thought of what I was going to do, and yes, it was right for me to do it!

Flying as fast as the car would go, all the things that had happened to me made me feel as if now I would be free! I reached to unbuckle the seat belt; I wanted no mistakes to stop me. My face still wet from the tears, I relaxed, clearing my mind of any regrets about what I was doing. I could see the tree on the curve ahead. I said, "Take me God, free me from the hell on earth! Who are you? NNNOOOOOOOOOOO! Get out of my way!" Hitting the brakes caused me to start spinning around. Suddenly, the car came to a halt half on the road and half in the ditch. I looked back where I had just been to see if someone was standing there. No one! Who was that? Picturing what I had seen, till this day I don't know who or what it was that caused me to hit the brakes. A white human form had faced me from the front of my car, putting their hand up to stop me, saying, "No don't do this, please don't." I just knew I had killed someone, but looking back, there was no one there. I went back to see if they were lying on the side of the road. There was no one there. I didn't know what had just happened; scared, I went back to my daughter's to tell her I was sorry and was going home. Never telling anyone what had happened; I didn't know the worst was yet to come.

A couple of months later, I began to have headaches that were so bad I couldn't stand up or eat. For days I held on to my pillow, crying, with the pain sometimes causing me to scream. Paul was so nice, bringing me coffee, coke, and orange juice in the mornings before he left, and in the evenings when he came home. I asked him time and time again, what was wrong with me? He didn't know, probably a virus. On the ninth day, Sonja came by. "Mom," she said, "if you're not better tomorrow, I'm taking you to a doctor." I told her to make an appointment now, because I was in so much pain that something terrible had to be wrong. The next day, she came for me, saying she had more things to do than to run me around. Looking at her, I wondered why I didn't just die. The doctor said he couldn't find anything wrong with me, but he gave me two prescriptions. The next morning I woke up with blood pouring from my nose. It was all over my face and pillow. "God? Is this the way I'm supposed to die?" Crying, I didn't know what to do. There was no one to help me, and the phone was moved. I didn't take any more of the pills. The bleeding stopped a day later.

Lying there alone, I wondered what could be making me so sick? I had not eaten anything for the last ten days. That night, the pain was worse than ever. As I slid my hands under the pillow to pull it around my head, my hand touched something. It was a gun that wasn't there before. With the pain increasing by the minute, looking at the gun in my hand, I checked for bullets, it was loaded. Cocking back the hammer, I put the barrel to the temple of my head. I was looking at Paul sleeping soundly in his room, while I sat there suffering. Just as I started squeezing the trigger, a voice said, "Don't do this. You don't believe in it." "But I'm hurting," I whispered. "It hurts. It won't stop!" I held the gun for several hours before I took it from my head. Drawing my knees up to me, gun still in my hand, I raised it up, pointing it at my husband. I thought, just let it go, shoot him; he's the one doing this! Again, the voice said, "You think you are in a prison now; if you shoot him, you'll be in a smaller prison." As it was getting daylight, I slid down under the covers and pretended to be asleep, listening to Paul as he got ready for work. After I heard him leave, I stared at the coffee, coke, and juice he had put on my nightstand. That was all that had entered my body since the headaches started. Dragging myself up, I washed the cup and glasses, after pouring out everything. I dried the sink and refilled the cup and glasses. My body was feeling so heavy and weak, as if I were dying. My wish? That evening he came in to fix my drinks, and went out to the back. I managed to get up and do the same thing again that I had done that morning. To my surprise, I felt a little better; not much, but just enough to balance myself. The next morning I did the same. With each passing day, I felt better. He had to be putting something in the drinks. If not, why was I feeling better? On the twelfth day, the headaches had subsided. Very little pain now. I was even a little hungry.

Paul came home to find me slowly walking around. He screamed at me, "What are you doing up? Get back into bed Marion; I'll make you some coffee." I let him, but when he went out, I dumped it, fixed more, and dried the sink so he couldn't see what I had done. The next day, I felt much like my old self. Again he came home screaming, "How is it you're up? You shouldn't be able to get up!" I looked at him and asked, "Why not Paul? Why is it I'm not supposed to be up?" Stuttering around, he told me I was sick. He asked me if I had been drinking the coffee. "Well, of course." He had a concerned look on his face, and shook his head, saying, "I just don't understand." Without a doubt, I knew he was trying to kill me. Often he made me coffee, without him knowing it got tossed out. Once he said, "Try your coffee, hope I made it right." Turning the cup up, the coffee only touched my lips enough to let him think I had taken some in; then I pretended to swallow. That's when I made up my mind to get out! I knew I had to get out before he killed me! Wheels of motion began to turn! I knew no one would help, no one would believe me, and no one cared. I had never let anyone know how he had beaten me for 28 years, mentally abused me and that I suspected he was putting d-con in my coffee. I think in the back of my mind I really didn't want to believe he would stoop so low as to do it. Who put this idea in his head?

My plans were made and I spoke to Sonja, of course she would drive me to the airport. When the time came she didn't show up. It made me wonder if she knew what Paul had been doing. I called her many times, but she wouldn't answer her phone. Why do people keep making decisions for me? Why? The only thing I knew to do was go to my half brother's house and see if his wife was home. She knew how it was and even said I needed to get away before he did hurt me. She was there but didn't want to drive me, I told her if she didn't go with me I would stomp her in the ground if I missed my plane. She went with me and drove the car back. Leaving everything but a few clothes, I took my first flight from home; so far away I knew he couldn't find me! Even today I look back and wonder how could I have been so stupid and naïve? My family and ex husband still thinks I'm that same person. Maybe I am, because I did go back a month later.

Courage to Leave

Each time I thought about leaving reminded me of the pain I received from the first attempt many years ago. One Friday night I couldn't deal with facing another day of my prison, especially facing another hungry weekend. Paul seemed not to care if we had any groceries or provisions for everyday life. He would take off Saturday mornings after he woke up, saying he was going to the store or hunting. He always came home five or six hours later empty handed, and each weekend he came home later and later. By accident, I found out he was going to his mother's to eat lunch and dinner, knowing we had nothing to eat. How could he? We had two little girls who needed food. So on this one Friday night I called a friend from my old neighborhood. She told me to come on; maybe Paul would wake up and see what he was doing to his family. She already had company, so I slept a couple of hours in a recliner. Dreading to face Paul again, I had coffee with my friend, and she told me I was welcome to come back any time. I drove the car home. Paul didn't say a word to me as he was hoeing the empty garden. The whole time vegetables were there he never touched it. I got out with my purse and told him I brought the car back to him because I knew he needed it to take the girls with him to his mother's to eat lunch and dinner. I said if he didn't, I wanted him to find food in the house to feed them! He had never been alone with our daughters before, never changed a diaper, and never even fed them.

I got nearly to the end of the gravel driveway when I heard something behind me. It was Paul running as fast as he could. I ran, but he caught me, grabbing my long hair and jerking me backwards. He started dragging me to the house with the gravel tearing my shirt, leaving long scratches on my back. Even though I was screaming, I could hear him yelling: "If you want to act crazy, then I'll treat you like a crazy person! You dumb, stupid bitch!!!" He dragged me all the way to the house with me screaming. I don't know what hurt the worst, him pulling my hair, the rocks on my back, or his words. Once we got there, slamming the door, he told me to fix lunch for them. Crying, screaming, I told him there was nothing. "Go look for yourself! Go! If you can find something for me to cook, then I will do as you ask!" He came out of the kitchen and handed me five dollars, saying for me to go to the service station three blocks away and buy groceries. I looked at him with tears running from my eyes. Five dollars? On my way out, he said to be sure and bring his change back. I did as I was told, bringing home dry beans, flour, lard, potatoes, and one pack of meat. He stayed home that day, but the next day he left, saying he was going squirrel hunting. I watched as he left and gave him 30 minutes. I called his mom's and said I wanted to speak to Paul. I heard him say: "Tell her I'm not here." She replied that I knew he was there. He answered the phone and asked how did I know he was there? In a calm voice, I said, "You are a pathetic liar, and it is easy to see you can't live without your parents." He said he'd come for us. He did, but for the next three months he would take us there every weekend and then just leave. When we were there, he never stayed; but when we were home, he stayed at his parents'. His mom would be oh so nice while he was there. After he was gone, she wouldn't speak. She and her daughter, Annie, would leave each room as I entered. I followed them outside and they would go in, and do just the opposite when I followed. Finally, after three months I couldn't take it anymore. My daughters and I stayed home. Paul said his mother never treated me that way.

I didn't try to leave again for a long time. It was around our twelfth anniversary when his dad gave one of Pauls's old girlfriends our phone number. He talked to her close to four hours. I knew by what he said that they were to meet, I never knew if they did or not. But I did know he had a girlfriend, and one day he came home and asked me if she could move in. How could he? This was our home with our daughters. I asked him if he wanted a divorce. He said, "No, this is my home." I wanted him to explain to me what made this his home. He didn't support us and never bought his daughters or me anything. He never paid the bills or bought any groceries. He was never at home when our daughters needed him. As a matter of fact, he was very seldom at home. So why did he think this was his home? He said, "I pay the rent, and that is why it is my home!" Eighty dollars a month! So why was it we never saw any of his paycheck? When I asked him to help with the bills, he would just laugh.

The night came when I couldn't deal with him, his girlfriends, or his absence after I found another woman's jeans and panties under our bed, not only that, there was a bullet hole in the wall by the dresser. He had been laid off from his job and had taken my car. When I got my paycheck, he demanded money every time I turned around, now he needed my car, since the bank had repossessed his truck. So each day he would take me to work two hours before time for me to clock in. The company I worked for didn't like it.

One day everything just crashed in on me about how much I did and why I was so tired. We had 63 animals and two acres of garden. I had one acre of grass cutting with a push mower, house cleaning, preparing their meals, shopping, my mother calling every day with her problems, my job, and my husband's demands. Also, I had the worry about my daughters, who couldn't understand why I wasn't home with them. It all hit me so hard. All I needed was a place to think clearly what I needed to do. My workmate, Betty, wasn't at work that night, but I managed to call her and see if she would come for me at nine o'clock. She did, and we talked about the situation. I asked if I could stay with her until Sunday night. No problem; I was welcome. It was her birthday and she was celebrating at a club. I told her it was okay, that I'd sit off to myself and try to find a way to resolve my problems. No one spoke to me the rest of the time, but I did order a beer. When I took a sip of the second one, in walked Paul. I don't know how he found me. He started screeching: "Where is he?" Confused, I only stared at him. He continued: "Is he in the bathroom, or did he run?" I asked, "Who are you talking about?" He left the table and returned with a beer. I explained to him about everything, and said if I could only have just a little time to myself, then maybe I could work it all out. I also asked him where had he been. He said it was none of my business. I just stared at him. He had half of my paycheck in his pocket, he had my car, he had left the girls alone, and he had no job. This was none of my business?

Closing time came for the club. I told him I was going home with Betty until Sunday, and then we could talk. He stared down at me and said, "Yeah, right!" As we entered the parking lot, I walked behind Betty, her boyfriend, sister and her husband. Paul grabbed me by the back of my coat, shoving me towards my car. I tried to get way from him, but he slammed me on the hood of the car, punching me violently in my face. Screaming, I tried to get away. He jerked me up and threw me inside of the car on my back. I kicked and screamed, but no one helped me. I knew if I didn't do something, he was going to kill me. I could taste the blood in my mouth, and I thought, "Dear God, I'm going to die!" I just burst out laughing and screamed, "Stop, stop, you're killing me!" He held me there until I promised to go home with him. Standing up, with blood running from my face all down the front of my white fur coat, I walked towards Betty's car. Can you believe the two women and two men in the car were scared so bad they locked the doors? Paul jerked me back and said, "That's far enough!" Betty rolled her window down a little and asked if I was okay.

I replied, "Look at me. Do I look okay? But you go on and don't worry about me; I have to go home with him!" When we got back to my car, he shoved me into the driver's side across the steering wheel, still holding on to me. We talked on the way home. I asked him why was it okay for him to be gone on his own all of the time? Why was it I never had any time to myself? Why? He said that I was his wife, and I was to do what he told me to; I had no freedom. As we pulled up in the driveway, I asked him what was the name of the woman that he had in my car? I could smell her cologne on him, and you could smell semen in the car. He parked the car and turned to talk to me. We sat there for a few minutes while he warned me if I did anything else like this, he would fix me. I reached for the keys and told Paul if he needed a whore car he should buy him one that our daughters wouldn't have to ride in. He grabbed my hand, squeezing the keys inside of it. He pushed my hand in between the seats and behind me until my arm gave off a loud POP! He said it didn't matter if I did pay for the car; it was HIS! Screaming, I begged him to stop! "You broke my arm!! Turn me loose, please!!!! Take the keys!!!! Let me go!!!!!" I had to reach back with my right hand to pull my left one up; I couldn't move it. Crying, I got out of the car and walked to the house holding my arm. He was already sitting in recliner with a beer. He said, "I bet you won't try to leave me again!" Saying nothing, I went to change my clothes and get the blood off of me. With my gown on, holding my swollen arm, I by-passed the living room and went straight to bed. Our daughters were spending the night with their friends from school, I didn't know it until I got home. It really scared me for them to be gone. Paul never hit me in front of them, and their daddy was their hero. I never let them know about the things he did to me. I was afraid if they did, he might start on them. Several times I saw him pull their hair or take his bony knuckles and pop them on the back of the head before I could get to them. As I told him, "You want to hit someone, hit me; but don't you ever hit my girls!"

My arm was hurting so bad, my face was swollen, and my ears were ringing. I whimpered quietly like a little puppy someone had kicked. I thought, "Oh no, here he comes to bed. I'll pretend to be asleep!" My back was to him as he lay down next to me. I just held my breath, feeling as if something was going to happen. He whispered, "I want to have sex with you." I didn't dare move; in hopes he'd think I was asleep. But when he put his hand on my shoulder, my whole body jerked hard like a seizure. The next thing I knew I felt a horrible hit to the right side of my head above the temple, and a pain in my back, as I went flying out of the bed up against the wall. I crumpled on the floor, only to wake up realizing he had knocked me out. I tried to get up by pulling on the dresser as he was screaming something that I couldn't hear for the ringing. The first thing I saw as I stood up was the reflection of myself in the mirror. I thought, "Oh God, what has he done to me?" My arm was black, my face had cuts on it, and oh how my head was hurting! I didn't know if I was going to die, but I knew I had a concussion from the huge white thing sticking out of my head right at the hairline. He had hit me with something! But what was it? I turned to focus on what he was saying, and then I saw it! He had his brass knucks on his hand! What had he intended to do to me with them when he came to bed? What? My back was hurting with all the rest of the pain. I tried to picture what had just happened. He had hit me on the head and kicked me out of bed with both of his feet. It had felt like an elephant had kicked me in my back. My eyes could see two of him jerking around, pulling his pants on. He was saying something about that he was going to get me a short dick! What was he talking about? I screamed for him to look at what he had done to me. He said he couldn't care less; he was leaving! As he left the bedroom, he screamed, "Next time I'll fix you for good!" I tried so hard to figure out what he was talking about. It didn't make sense. He had totally lost it in his own little world. It took me a few minutes to get outside to see if he was gone. He usually went to the Waffle House to meet his girlfriend, I think that is where she worked. I didn't know and really didn't care. I had been there with his picture, saying I was his sister and I couldn't find him. But no one recognized him, so I let it go. When I got outside, he was coming back up the driveway going towards the garden, doing donuts with my car, and screaming as loud as he could. I couldn't understand him, so I thought this was the right time to get it over with. I thought, "Just let him kill me; I can't take this anymore. Everything I did was wrong in his eyes, I just don't want to live. My girls will be okay, maybe better off without me." I went through the double gate and stood right in the middle of the drive where he couldn't pass without hitting me. Spread-eagled, I waited as he raced the motor. I stared right into his eyes, thinking, "This is it! The pain, the suffering, the hell, they're over!!" Driving the car straight at me, he saw that I wasn't going to move. He slammed on the brakes and slid into me, trying to stop. With the bumper against my stomach, I never even flinched, still staring at him. With his face as white as a ghost, he sat there in shock that he had not even knocked me down. Looking at him, my mouth opened, asking: "Is that the best you can do Paul? You're nothing but a coward! Back it up; do it again, but this time do it right!!!! I'd rather be dead than to live with you! You are not my mother, my owner, or anything else to me! You only fathered my daughters. You're not even a father to them, but you will have to be if I'm not here! Now do it!!!! You low-life, poor excuse for a human! Where are your guts now? Come on! Back it up! No, wait, I'll back it up. Reverse might be too hard for you to understand!" Backing up, I screamed, "Gas the damn car!!!!!!!! Hit me!!! For God's sake, let me die!!!" My heart had turned stone cold to Paul as I watched him get out of the car crying. He came towards me and I stepped back, saying not to touch me. The rest of the night I couldn't go to sleep in fear of what he might do.

The next morning I had a hard time trying to move around. The white bulging knot had shrunk a little. I had to find a bandage to put on my arm, and tie a sling around my neck to hold it up. Around ten a.m. Casey called, saying they were coming home. When they arrived, their first question was, "What happened, Mommy?" Paul said, "Oh, she had a little too much to drink and fell in the driveway." Then he laughed. I looked at him, shaking my head, thinking, "God, what a liar he is; anything to keep them from knowing what he did to me!" At the same time, I didn't want to destroy the love my girls had for their father.

It took many years before I tried to get away again. I worked constantly to keep away from Paul. Then we moved to the country. We only went camping once, and he beat me to a pulp the first night. I still don't know why he did it. I was afraid to be alone with him again for years. So many times I wanted to get away. He had me right where he wanted me for the next 14 years. Until one day I ran, ran as hard as I could! With all of my heart, I knew I had to get as far as I could away from him before he destroyed me completely! He vowed to me he would kill me if it were the last thing he ever did! I have no doubt in my heart that I would not be here writing these stories today if I had stayed with him.

Last Time

The first week after I left, I called my daughters to let them know that I was okay. The only concern they had was their daddy wanted to talk to me. It was fine with me; I'd call Paul later when he was home from work. In a way, it was funny to hear his voice sounding different. Answering all of his questions with yes or no, I reminded him of my prediction several years before, what I would do if he and the girls didn't straighten up. At this time Paul didn't know that I knew he had poisoned me. I reminded him that when I was so sick and he wouldn't take me to the hospital a few months before that really showed me how much he hated me. Denying everything, he said he wished I had taken my car, I had no idea what he meant by that. He had given my truck away and traded my car off, then sold my quad runner the second day after I left. Since I had never been away from home more than two weeks at one time, it didn't take me long to want to go back. The only way possible to make this work was to get Sonja to come for me at the bus station. She gave me her word of honor not to tell Paul I was coming home. That way I could get my old job back, get a place to stay, and get a way to travel. No more fussing, arguing, or life-threatening situations. That should work out fine. Sonja and her boyfriend, Jacob showed up at the airport. We were excited to see each other, and chatted all the way to her home. Maybe this time my daughter and I could be close once again.

Not five minutes after we walked in the door, Paul pulled up. My mouth flew open, my heart beating so hard I was shaking! I screamed at my daughter, "HOW COULD YOU, AFTER WHAT HE DID TO ME? HOW? I TRUSTED YOU!" Her little-girl voice said, "I had to, Mommy, I had to; he's my daddy!" Betrayed by my own daughter! Looking at her, trying to control myself, I asked her, "What the hell gives you the right to control my life? After all of the things you've done? Why? I don't understand; you want him to kill me?"

Paul came in the door and there was nowhere for me to run, no exit; I was trapped! What was I going to do? I knew he would try to kill me again. I couldn't trust anyone! Sonja said we had to leave. Asking her why, she replied that I was his wife and supposed to be with him. I looked at my daughter with a disgusted look that showed her she had betrayed my trust. I gritted my teeth at her, saying, "I hope you are happy now!" That was the one and only time I ever hated her in my life!

On the way to the house, he tried to hold my hand, I don't know why. There was no way for me to run again. Why was this happening to me? I just kept quiet to see how he was going to try again. Our first night back together, he stayed by my side. Even when I went to the bathroom, he would sit outside the door. At bedtime, he pressed up against me in my old bed. I couldn't go to sleep until I heard him breathing heavy.

The next morning he told me I could use his truck, and laid twenty dollars on the table. He asked what I was going to do for the day. Maybe I would go see my older sister, Carmen. After he left, I decided to go shopping. I did, and rode around, then went back to the house. I didn't talk to anyone, for I had one thing on my mind, when is he going to try again, when? I looked at everything in the house I had worked so hard for. What had happened in one month with the house? It looked nothing like it did when I left, so different now. It was meaningless. Right then it dawned on me. All the work, remodelling, decorating, painting, and building meant not a thing to me. It wasn't worth the effort, money, and time I had spent, trying to get the abuse to stop while waiting for approval from the one man I had once loved so dearly. Most of my clothes were gone: the suits, shoes, and accessories. It felt like I was visiting someone, not a place I once lived. I laid the change from the twenty dollars on the kitchen table. Turning on the television, I thought, "Well, so far so good." I knew he was going to do something, but I had no idea what, that really scared me. When it was time for him to come home, he banged the door open in a rage! "Where's my money? If you think you're going to run half-way across the country on my money in my truck, you're crazy as hell!" I moved closer to the door, telling him his change was lying on the table with his keys. I had used part of the money to get some film developed. He continued to scream at me, "You didn't go to your sister's today! You lying bitch!" I watched him as he continued screaming. He finally snatched a beer from the fridge. He sounded like a raging bull, the way he was snorting. I was too afraid to move from the door, waiting for him to come after me. He went out the back door, slamming it, as I sat back down. A minute later, he came back in and I jumped for the door. He asked me if I wanted to go out dancing. "Me? You've never asked before." Well, he said, "I'd like for you to meet some of the women I've been dating." I told him it was ok; he could go without me and meet them if he wanted; it didn't bother me anymore. But he insisted that I go. I couldn't believe what he had been dating; no wonder he thought I was so good looking. I watched him as he was dancing with several different women. He kept looking to see if I was looking, I wasn't. Later, my half-brother Gary and his wife, Lisa Anne came in. He asked me to dance, and we laughed, having a good time. I recognized another woman that had come in, as she was trying to get into a dark corner. I knew she was Gary's neighbor. I wondered why she was staying in the dark. Later, Paul asked me to dance; sure, why not? Then I saw the woman in the dark leaving, very angry. That was strange! I've known her for years. Later I found out why she was ignoring me.

Paul took Gary, Lisa, and myself out to dinner. He had never done that before, I always had to pay. He kept buying me drinks, but I never let them out of my sight. That night, after we got home, he started kissing on me, laying me back on the bed so gently. I thought, how could he do this, after all he had done to me? As I was trying to get up, he said we were going to start over. Knowing he had been with those other women, I couldn't let him touch me. I think deep inside I was afraid my feelings would forget it all and love him again. He knew just how to work me, because he had done it so many times before. I let him go as far as I dared to. All of a sudden it struck me as funny, could it be that my body was actually responding to him? One way, I wanted the love we used to have; another way, I was afraid that I would end up in the abuse again. The only thing I could do was start laughing out loud, knowing it could be dangerous, since he had me trapped on the bed. I asked him did he really think he was turning me on? Tears poured out of his eyes, begging, "Please, please, don't do this!" Pushing him off of me, I knew I'd better get to where I could run if I needed to. I went outside and he followed, saying he knew it would take time, but it would be better this time. We would go slowly. Time went by, but the more that passed the more I knew I had made a mistake coming back. The next day was Sunday, rising up early I made my coffee, and went out to the front steps, asking myself why I had come back. "What am I looking for? I don't belong here, and I didn't feel as if I belonged in the other state. Do I belong anywhere?" Not long after that, Paul came out the door with his coffee. As soon as I finished, he offered to make a cup for me. My heart went to triple speed. Taking a deep breath, I said sure, that would be nice. I gave him time to fix our coffee, slipped up quietly, stepped inside, and watched him. Walking very quietly up behind him,

I asked, "What are you doing?" He jumped as if I had shot him, saying, "I'm making our coffee; what does it look like I'm doing?" Looking at him, and remembering the headaches, I said, "Here, a new beginning so let's do something different. You drink my coffee, and I'll drink yours." He tried to get his cup from me. I said, "No, you drink mine, please; and here, you can put milk and sugar in it if you want." He said I was on drugs and as crazy as they come. I told him I knew what he had done with the poison. "You're crazy!" he screamed! Going to the sink with my cup, I told Paul to watch. If there was nothing in my cup, he could do anything to me he wanted; but if there is something, then it would be my turn. He kept walking away. I said, "Look, what is this, Paul?" No answer. "Paul? It's green grains in the bottom of my cup! You really poisoned me! I should call the police!" He said to go ahead, and he would tell them I did it myself! Stupid me, why did I have to pick the cup up? "Can you tell me why you poisoned me? Can you tell me why you drugged me? Talk to me!" I demanded. His words from before came out of his mouth: "I told you I would kill you before I let you go!" But why Paul, you don't love me, you're always with other women, talk to me, tell me why? Something clicked inside of me, and I'm not afraid to say people a mile away could hear me. He looked so scared of me, and then he ran to the door. I actually had him on the run! He heard me yelling everything I knew about him: the girlfriends, dating my sisters, my friends, the drugs, and the poisonings! He ran back through at one point to grab the phone. It didn't matter to me who he called, as long as I could get away from him. While he was on the phone, I said not one word, just waited, listening to him talk. He didn't have time to put the phone back after he hung it up. A big burst of adrenaline hit me as I turned to him, saying, "You are mine now, after all of these years of hell and abuse you have put me through! YOU ARE MINE!" Darting after him, with everything he ever did to me in my mind, I thought I would kill him if I could catch him! Tired of trying to catch him, I started throwing anything I could find to throw. I finally went in the house to pack my luggage. He wasn't worth it!

As I packed, he was unpacking what I had packed. He told me I had to leave with nothing but the clothes on my back. Sonja came in; her dad went on to explain how crazy I was and that I was on some kind of drugs. I winked and smiled at her. I managed to get some of my clothes, while she was saying, "I think you need to go home with me, Mom." The obedient person I am, we left, only for me to end up going to another state.

Liar, Liar

It was December after our divorce; I sat on my sofa holding the phone, with scalding tears flowing down my cheeks. I had received a call from Sonja three days earlier. "Mom, Daddy wants to talk to you; I think he's going to tell you he wants you to come home. He'll call you Friday night at six." I asked, "Does he still love me?" "Yes," she replied. Thinking my now ex-husband still loved me, I thought it over all I had been through in the last few months. The little inkling of hope in my mind thinking that with me gone for the past few months, just maybe it would be different when I go back this time. But how could I live on guard all of the time, never knowing what he's going to try next. My first Thanksgiving without my family nearly killed me with the emptiness in my heart. Now with Christmas coming, how will I ever deal with it, I must go back, I need my daughters and grandchildren. Whatever he does I'll just have to live or die with it. I'm going home!

I packed, emptied my bank account, and informed my landlord and employer that I was leaving in three days. All set to drive a thousand miles back home to my family, waiting for six o'clock to come. At five forty, the phone rang. Happy, singing, I ran to answer, thinking it was a friend calling to say I would be missed and to have a safe trip. The voice on the phone was someone I recognized, and I asked, "Why are you calling me at this time?" The voice said, "I know you will talk to Paul at six tonight. I just couldn't let you walk into his trap. What I am about to tell you will hurt, and I'm so sorry. I can't stand by and watch him hurt you more than he has already." The voice went on to tell what she knew to be the truth. The hot tears of pain ran down my face as I listened. Then I asked the voice on the phone, "Are you sure this is true?" Yes, I am positive!" replied the voice. In shock from the new news, all I could say was, "Thank you," and hung up the phone. I knew in a few minutes the phone would ring. I waited. "Must have control; I can say I have a cold," I thought, composing myself for the call. At 6:05, the phone still had not rung. Ten, fifteen minutes passed, no call. There was nothing for me to wait for so I called my daughter, but it was Paul that answered . . . .

Oh, how sweet and loving his voice was. "I miss you babe; please come home." He didn't even notice I had been crying; he just continued talking. "If we can't live together, we'll get you an apartment, and we can start over, date, and get reacquainted with each other. Don't you want to come home? Our daughters need their mom, please come home!" I listened to his begging pleas, crying his heart out to me. "Oh my love, please come home! You do still have my money and truck from the divorce, don't you? Please, please come home! I'll do anything for you if you'll just come home." I listened to him with no tears flowing, only anger building. I asked him was he sure he wanted me to come home? "Yes! Yes!" he answered. Without thinking, I asked, "Will you tell our daughters that you poisoned their mom with arsenic for nine days?" "Now, I don't know about that," he replied. "But anything to get you to come back." I couldn't believe he finally admitted to the poisoning. "Let's see how far he'll go," I thought. I continued, "Will you tell them you cut the brake line on their mom's truck?" "Yes, babe, please come home," he was still begging. I listened to him as he babbled on and on. Using this time to think, I was ready to end the conversation with: "LIAR! You'll never tell our daughters the truth!"

Let's just see if he'll tell me the truth. I said that I was still single and asked if he was. "Yes, babe, there will never be anyone else for me, only you!" he cried, sobbing. Paul what are you crying for, is Sonja in there with you? He said yes. I knew then he was putting on a show for her. He'll never change, what am I thinking? Let's see if he'll tell me the truth. "Paul. I have one more question for you". With a smile on my angry face, I asked him, "Can you tell me what your NEW WIFE has to say about sharing you with me?" He screamed so loud in my ear that I dropped the phone, "How did you know about HER?"

After Liar, Liar

As I dropped the phone, my tears flowed as never before. My heart had dropped to my stomach. How could I have been so stupid as to even believe Paul loved me? Shaking, crying, with so much pain in my chest, I thought, "What am I to do? Who am I to trust? There's no one for me." The thoughts that were going through my mind told me not to stay there alone; I had get out. My chest kept feeling as if it would explode. I went to the grocery store for a few things and a lot of beer. My plans were to lock myself up and not see or trust anyone again. When I returned, the phone was still lying on the floor. As I touched it, I couldn't get my breath. I grabbed my purse and went out the door. I knew that I didn't need to be alone. One thought in my mind scared me, while the other thoughts were rational. Stay alone, and die alone.

The club was only three blocks away, and I knew I wouldn't be able to drive later, so I walked. The feeling inside of me needed to come out. Was it pain, or was it anger? I could still hear his words in my head. "I love you, please come home!" Looking at my door card as it slid through the slot to enter the club, I was wondering what to say as I entered. It was nearly empty, except for a few regulars. No one was sitting at the tables close to the dartboard. So I chose a table, and the waitress brought me my regular drink. I looked at her, saying, "Don't let my glass be empty!" The more I threw the darts, the harder I threw, and the higher my score. Why won't his voice get out of my head??? Hot, boiling tears scalded my face. The darts flew harder and harder! A few beers later, the waitress walked up to me, putting her hands on my shoulders and looking me straight in the eyes, I couldn't speak. She said, "Please tell me what terrible thing has happened to you, Marion. This isn't like you. I think of you as my mother. You're always happy, with a beautiful smile on your face. Please, won't you tell me what happened?" I picked her up by her blouse, looking straight into her eyes. A deep angry voice came out of my mouth, saying, "The best thing you can do is get the hell away from me now! Now! Or you will get hurt!" No one came near the dartboard or me until some hours later. I could hear voices mumbling. "Come on, let us take you home, you'll be okay." The waitress had called two of my friends, Peggy and Daniel, to come for me; she had never seen me like this. All I remember is them unlocking my door, and remembered Peggy saying: "Go to sleep, it will be better tomorrow." Daniel said, "We'll lock the door on our way out." They both were asking each other if I had said anything about what had happened to me. They knew nothing. I cried till I fell asleep.

For three days, I never left my duplex apartment. The phone would ring until I could no longer stand it. Shutting it off that first morning made me remember the last conversation I had on it. Opening the fridge, but not wanting anything to eat, I reached for a beer. I'd drink, sleep, drink, and sleep for the next three days. I remember at one point I started screaming, never stopping until my voice went hoarse. I wanted to die! As I lay on the sofa, a sharp pain hit me in my chest. Not being able to breathe, I accepted it as my death wish. Why doesn't anyone love me? Why? I can't stand being alone. I knew not what God's plans were for me, but I didn't die. Later, I found out it was the first of six mild strokes. I managed to go back to work. After two weeks, I went back to the club. Peggy asked me to sit at the bar; she wanted to buy me a drink. After we talked for a while, I was able to talk to her what had happened, but not without crying. She asked, "After all of the years you spent with him, how could he still be so cruel to you?" Better yet Marion, how could you be so naïve and let yourself off guard? Without waiting for an answer, she went on to ask me what I would do now. Looking around at the people in the club, I shook my head and said, "I have no idea, but I know this is no life for me. I don't belong here." Even today, five years later, my chest still hurts from that day. Will I ever learn to stop trusting, caring, or loving? I don't know how to stop, and it continues. I want to belong, I need to be needed, I need someone to care about me . . . .

Dedicated to My Guardian Angel

Beginning a new life in another state wasn't easy. For me it was lonesome and scary to be so far from home. In the meantime, I waited to hear from the jobs I had applied for. Then one day a lady came by, walking very fast. She did this several days a week at the same time. A few days later, she stopped and introduced herself as Dana. We exchanged names, and with that, she invited me to walk with her. I asked why she walked so fast? She said, "Marion, if I walked fast for twenty minutes, it would be the same as if I walked for two hours at a regular pace." We enjoyed the walk together, sometimes stopping to discuss the different styles of houses in the neighbourhood.

As I got to know Dana, it seemed that we had a lot in common. Our friendship was a connection we both could feel, but she was a very sick lady who had spent most of the past ten years in bed. She explained many things about her sickness. We talked about our families and why I had moved there. Then she told me about her husband, Stephen, he was a preacher, and took care of their rental houses. But he didn't seem to have time for her, even when she just needed a good hug. Dana said I hugged with love. She could feel it, and sometimes she scared me, holding on so long. It had been along time since anyone hugged me with so much compassion. But I know now that I was giving her what she missed at home.

Dana invited me to dinner one night. Their house seemed strangely decorated with farm tools, which came from her fathers' farm. It was neat and clean, but you wouldn't expect to see one decorated like this, especially in such a high class maintained neighbourhood. The meal was even more so strange. There was not enough food for one person, much less the four of us, her son, Brad, had came home for the weekend. Next to their plates were 11 to 14 pills, more or less. Jokingly, I asked if they were dope addicts. They just laughed and said no, it was vitamins. They each took one to two tablespoons of food from each small bowl. I just waited until they finished, but I only took one spoon from each dish. The meat was spoiled with a sickening odor. I couldn't eat it. They asked if something was wrong. Not wanting to hurt their feelings, I just said that I wasn't very hungry.

She would call me frequently to come and visit, and I would sit in a rocker as we talked, until she fell asleep. Often she would have small seizures; all you could do was sit and talk to her. More than once, Dana would tell me how good it made her feel for us to talk about things we liked. When spring came, it was hard for her to go outside. For some reason, she was horrified of the birds, and would go into a panic on the ground. It was hard to get her to do anything except when she wanted. The more I watched her, the more I wondered if she was physically or mentally ill. On the night of the dinner, as I watched, she and Brad had a disagreement. Stephen agreed with him on the subject. Then she went from completely normal to being sick, and back to normal; she was pretending. I saw it, and Dana knew it. I just kept quiet, and she stopped calling for a while.

Several months later, she called, saying she knew of several yard sales in the neighborhood, and asked if I'd walk with her. Now you've got to picture this: she lived in a huge house that cost $200,000, more or less. As we looked around at the second-hand merchandise, Dana picked up a lady's wallet; six times she did this, asking me several times, if it were me, would I buy it? I said, "Very nice wallet, sure I would, and the name brand is very expensive. Buy it, Dana!" She didn't. Twice she walked back to it after we walked away. I felt a little guilty for not buying it for her. If I only had the money, what little change I had I spent on some very nice clothing and I apologized to her. She ranted on, did I think Stephen would give her the money, was it too expensive, she would really love to have it. We stopped and I looked her straight in the eye. I told her, "My God, girlfriend! It's only 25 cents! What goes on in your household?" She didn't answer. With a disappointed look on her face, she said, "I never have any cash, so why should I buy a wallet?" This lady, who was very educated, who had been a principal for years at a school, and who had studied psychiatry, would not spend 25 cents for herself. What kind of life was she living? I begin to believe Stephen was a controlling person.

We continued our walk, and I asked if Dana would slow down; "You're killing me by walking so fast." She said, "Don't worry Marion; I'm going to die before you, maybe in a year." I felt a weird feeling in my chest, making me feel as if she was telling the truth. On impulse, I told her she would outlive us all. She stopped and said, "No my friend, no I won't. I will be dead in a year." So with that she hooked her arm around mine and we continued our walk in silence. Then I felt very compelled to tell her about the previous experiences of life after death after my mother and sister had passed. She said if it were true, she would visit me. Since she had to stay in bed so much, which was where she would contact me. She stooped down running her finger from my foot and saying she would be crawling up to my heart, she touched my chest. She made it a point that I had better be alone. She said, "I will be your Guardian Angel, Marion! If anyone ever needed a Guardian Angel, it is you!" Dana said, "Marion, I've never met anyone that has as much bad luck as you." Before we arrived back home, she told me that her family had had enough of her being sick, and that her three children had moved from home to different states, to attend college and live their own lives. She said, "Stephen has showed me in many ways that he doesn't love me." I tried so hard to convince her that he did love her. We both grew silent, and then we parted our ways.

Later I went to work, and problems began where I was staying, and Dana had called right in the middle of a huge argument and requested me to move in with her. It would relieve her mind of being a problem to Stephen. Many times she had expressed the lonesome depression she felt. So I thought I could help her to put her mind on new projects. Maybe I could stop her from thinking of things I knew she would not talk about to others. Stephen knew nothing of the things we talked about, but he had his own ideas of ruling my life, as he apparently did for her. He told me I was causing Dana problems. Later that night, she came to me after he left the house and apologized, saying she could do nothing. Because she had to do all Stephen told her to do. I ask why? She said it was in the Bible that she had to obey Stephen.

The next day, he dumped me at a shelter for women, bag and baggage. It caused a problem trying to get to work on time, because I didn't know where I was. The women there were thieves, drug addicts, prostitutes, and alcoholics. Every day, the women were arguing with each other. I worked two jobs: 5 a.m. till 11 a.m., then my second job started at 3 p.m. till 9 p.m. My first morning out I got so lost, I had walked nearly a mile from where I worked. After work, the leaders of the shelter assigned me to mopping the whole house and cleaning the showers. Later, even though I ate no food in that nasty place, they left all the dishes for me to wash from the 23 people who were living there. Only one other woman worked. The rest sat and watched TV until 2:00 or 3:00 in the mornings. Every night the chores became more and more. About two weeks later, I talked to one of the leaders, and all but one of the chores were assigned to the other women.

With no sleep, two jobs, night—time chores, exhausted and ready to drop, I had to get out! I could tell they had rambled in my luggage, I didn't know if anything was missing or not. Every night I cried until I fell asleep.

A month later I rented an apartment from Dana and Stephen, I didn't know anyone else to find a place to stay. With two jobs and Stephen's help, I knew I could handle it. Wrong! He took almost every penny I had, with nothing left for food, much less for anything else. Lord, help me! Nasty bugs! It took me more than two months before I could stand to take my clothes from my luggage. I couldn't even sleep in the bed for the stench.

Almost three months after I moved in, the neighbor, Emily, from next door came over. She seemed nice, but nosey, she wanted to compare our apartments. After seeing the kitchen, she stopped, looking at me with her hands on her hips saying, "That's what I thought!" Pulling my arm to her apartment, she fixed me a plate of food. She said, "EAT! You've lost too much weight since you moved in; why haven't you told someone that you needed food." It was because I was ashamed, ashamed to say I had to give all my money to the landlord. Then she gave me a few household things to use, also a radio. I returned the things Emily had loaned me after my divorce. I then had my own, and I didn't need hers anymore. The bugs were gone, my new home looked very nice, I could even sleep in my own bed. Dana, Stephen, and Brad visited a couple of times and she couldn't believe what a change in my apartment. Once I fixed them grilled cheese sandwiches and gave them Dr. Pepper to drink, when Stephen walked in, Dana ranted and raved over having a real Dr. Pepper saying, Marion can afford real drinks. It was strange, maybe Stephen was a money hoarder, I don't know, they had plenty but never used it. Then, about a year later, I found a house that I wanted to live in. I told Stephen; he just said, good luck. I asked him, what do I need to do to get my deposit back. He said I had to clean the apartment from top to bottom. My thoughts were, I had to clean the apartment after I moved. When I moved, I waited a month before

I called Stephen to say I was waiting for my deposit return of $200. He said there was no way I would receive it, that I had to give him a month's notice. I cried, screamed, and told him how God would get even with him. I told Stephen, "You will lose something more valuable than $200! You can't do people this way, but I know now how you got so RICH, but how can you call yourself a CHRISTIAN!" With that I hung up the phone.

With my jobs, and still decorating my little house, time just flew by. Even though I thought of Dana, I never called her. Before I moved she had met the man that moved in with me and begged me to get rid of him, she didn't like him, neither did I but he had no place to live. Sometime later Dana called twice; once while I was at work so I returned her call after I came home. Stephen answered, saying she was in bed and I couldn't speak with her. A few days later, she called again on my job, asking me to please call her on my day off, which was the next day; strange, but she requested a specific time when Stephen wasn't at home. When I called, we talked more than two hours, during the conversation, several times I felt as if someone kicked me in my stomach. To keep from worrying, I wrote it off as if she was having a bad day, but she never called me again.

It was in the year 2000, around the last of July. My roommate, Kelvin, needed a ride to his weekend job of cultivating huge cattle pastures, so I drove him there. When we rounded the first corner to the first red light, I stopped until it turned green. When I pressed the gas pedal, my car would not move! Kelvin asked, "What are you waiting on!" I told him my car wouldn't move and I pressed harder! Then I saw a car speeding from my left. After it flew by, my car started rolling. I asked myself what had stopped my car. The speeding car that never slowed for the red light would have killed us both. What was going on? The next weekend, another strange thing happened. I took Kelvin to do his field job, offering to bring him lunch. When I returned he was so far out that I decided to walk out to meet him. He came up and said he still had a little more to do before he could stop to eat, then he asked if I'd like to ride with him. I thought, why not? As I climbed up to the second step, the tractor lurched forward. To my right, the huge tire was just inches from my face. I felt two hands grip under my arms, carrying me up and out more than 15 feet, landing on the ground. What had just happened? Kelvin was as white as a ghost, not saying a word. We both knew I could have just been killed. Later I asked him if he knew what had happened. He didn't want to talk about it.

The third week I took him to work, the traffic light was green. I slowed to turn left and he began screaming, "WHOA, WHOA! LOOK OUT!" A big black, 4-wheel-drive SUV vehicle came flying at us right through his stoplight. I tried to go faster to the right side of the highway, but when I looked in my rear view mirror above the dash, there the black monster was on the back of my car! His front tires were up on my trunk! I braced myself waiting for the impact! Kelvin was still screaming, he's going to hit us! When I opened my eyes, the vehicle had passed us. I pulled into a parking lot, shaking, barely able to speak. What had just happened? I had seen the thing on the back of my car! Kelvin was just sitting there, not saying a word. Calming down I pulled out to continue to take him to work. When he came home that night, I told him he had to move out; I was sorry, but I couldn't take him to work anymore. He said, "Marion, I have no place to go." I told him he made more money than I did and he needed to get out. Three strikes, it was a warning for me. In a week, he had rented a small house not far away. I never took him to work again even though he would ask.

My house was clean, my cat, Sheena was fed and brushed, and to relax I decided to take a long, hot bath and go to bed early. Sheena slept with me, so before I went to sleep, I thought it was her at my feet under the covers. I kicked and told her to lie down. After the third or fourth time, I rose up; it wasn't her, she was lying right behind my back sound asleep. Then what moved my covers at my feet? When I was almost asleep, the covers moved again. I checked behind me and Sheena was still asleep. So I kept very still and waited; the covers moved again at my feet. My heart was racing, and I managed to say aloud: "I don't know who you are or what you are trying to tell me, but do what you need to do." The covers moved at my feet, and I watched as it continued to move up my legs, across my stomach, and then it stopped at my heart. I felt at peace with the movement. The more I thought about it, the more I got worried. I started calling people, family and friends. I knew someone had died, but who was it? Who saved my life? Who touched my heart? It had to be someone that cared about me. Giving up, I concentrated on work. A few days later, on my telephone ID, there was Dana's phone number. My thought was that maybe Stephen would give me my money. Oh great, I'll call him, but there was no answer. Later, he returned my call. Not meaning to sound rude, I came up front with, "What do you want, Stephen?" He said, "I don't know if you know or not, but Dana has died." What? How? He said she had hung herself in their bathroom about six weeks earlier. The conversation she and I had had a little more than a year before came to me, with all of the recent things that had happened. "That's it! She is the one that died!" I exclaimed almost to a scream. I heard myself laughing out loud. Stephen was crying, and I felt no pity for him. I reminded him what I had said about the money. Still crying, he asked how I could be so cruel, laughing about her death. "Stephen, I'm sorry, I'm not laughing about her death, but laughing about the strange things that has happened since she died, and explained all that had happened." His sobs became stronger as he asked, "Why didn't she come to me and not to you?" "Easy," I said, "she knew you didn't love her. She was planning this for a long time Stephen, and she knew you were hell-bent on getting away from her every day, which was why she came to me. She knew I loved her!" "And I still love you, my Guardian Angel! Thank you for being there for me!" There is life after death! Now I know you believe what I told you.

Talk to your friends and family about contacting each before death comes, you will see that it is true. Tell each other what you will do to let each other know that you made it to the Kingdom of Heaven. Don't wait until it's to late. Many people have felt things after one's death, but are afraid to say anything in fear of being thought insane. I have felt a temperature drop in a room to freezing, I have smelled scents, I have seen things move. Since Dana committed suicide, I think she had to make restitution for it. It wasn't time for me to die yet and she saved me. Guardian Angels are REAL!

Snakes!

It's amazing how things that happen in the past reflect on your future. When I was pregnant with my first daughter, I chased frogs and anything that came in front of me. But when I was pregnant with my second one, my husband, Paul, my mom, step dad, brother, Gary, little sister, Sophie, and I were in the mountains looking for blueberries. I put my hand up on a huge rock to balance myself. Mother screamed and scared me so bad I almost passed out, since my baby was due any time. There was a rattler coiled with his head up and tail shaking just inches from my hand. My step dad in front of me grabbed my arm and jerked me away from the rock. Paul caught me to keep me from falling. I was trying to get over the shock of the screaming and jerking as I watched Paul and step dad killing the poor snake. When it was over, they were both exhausted. My step dad said, "if that don't beat it, my pistol is in my pocket." They had stoned the poor thing to death. The snake had 14 rattlers and a button.

Years after my second daughter, Sonja, was born, that poor girl couldn't stand the thought of a snake being around her. But my first daughter, Casey, has never been afraid of anything and neither have I. Casey started collecting snakes when she was seven years old. Let me tell you, I was in shock the day I came home and discovered she had stopped at the bridge on her way home from school, to get a rattler and a water moccasin, and she had found a garden snake also. She put them in jars, and they lived in my kitchen, sitting on the chest freezer for a long time.

Paul hated to go berry picking with me; he said I drew snakes to myself. To him it was a bad omen. Everywhere I went, there were snakes next to me. One day I was picking huckleberries from a bank, when Paul said, "I'm going to walk down to the creek. Will you watch for the snakes?" I told him to go on, it was okay. When he came back, he said: "Don't move! Can't you see that snake?" When I looked where he said, I swear I couldn't see the thing. He told me the color of it and how many inches it was from my hand. There the little thing was. I said, "Oh well, he wants some berries also." Moving over so the snake had plenty of room, I continued to pick berries for the pie I could already smell. My rule is to never take every berry, always leave some for the creatures of the forest. Paul told me I had to be crazy; I asked why? He said, "You're not afraid of anything." I bit my lower lip and never said a word. My thought kept to myself that I am afraid of some thing, him!

There's only been twice I have felt any fear from a snake. The first time was when we were in our summer house, just getting the place ready to live in. I wanted to make a flower garden on the small bank at the back. The only things I could use to line my flowerbed, were rocks I collected. So I'd go down to the field at the left of the house. About my third trip down, I stepped on something that felt spongy. Thinking it was a rotten log, but confused at why hadn't I stepped on it before, since I was going the same way. On my way back I asked myself where did the log go? Was it a log? I froze solid in my tracks. The brush was about three feet high, and my arms were full of rocks. I couldn't speak or move, when I saw the snake standing with his head above the sagebrush. I was so scared I couldn't even breathe. Paul was on the other side of the house splitting firewood, with his back to me. I knew not to move. I stared at Paul so hard, he later said it felt like I touched him. But while I was staring, the only thought that came to my mind was: "If you love me at all, I know you can feel me." When he turned around, he dropped the axe and ran to the porch for his walking stick. As he ran, he looked into my eyes and followed them to the ground. The snake's head was as big as your hand is wide. He saw the snake before he got to me. With one swing of the stick, he killed it. I felt so bad about it afterwards that I cried. It was over seven feet long, only a rat snake! When we moved into the old house, it had two fireplaces, but only used one. About a year later we found several rattler skins in the unused fireplace. It didn't bother us, so we let it live there in peace.

Several years later after we had moved back to the city, we headed for the mountains where we were riding our quad runner in the rough part of the country, looking for blackberries. It was so bad that you couldn't get off for the mud and growth. But we went further to a logging road, and came to a huge mud hole. We knew it was deep, so I had to get off and go through the thick woods while he was on one knee to run the quad through and not get too muddy. But he couldn't get to the other side, because the mud hole was much deeper than we had thought and the woods were too thick. Then he wanted me to come back. I told him the down side was too deep in mud for me; he said: "Come back the way you just went."

Now anyone who lived in rattler country knew the rules: Never step over a log; you step on it, then jump away from it. The major thing was, you NEVER back-tracked on the same trail. I KNEW that, and I told Paul. We both knew the rules, but he said, "Come on, Marion, I'll watch for you." I couldn't see where I was stepping going back, and all of a sudden he screamed out, "STOP! STOP! STOP! DON'T PUT YOUR FOOT DOWN! STOP! BE STILL AND LISTEN!!!" I sucked in my breath and listened. Oh God, where was it??? I could hear the rattlers! I was holding one foot up and balancing on the other. Paul said: "Don't move or put your foot down, Marion." I changed the expression on my face. I guess he understood, because he said, "It's a huge rattler right under your foot, just inches away." My eyes opened wide as if asking what I was to do. He said I would have to jump backwards as far as I could. My eyes talked for me again. He knew there was no way I could go backwards. So he tried to draw the snake to him. When he got its attention, he said, "JUMP NOW!!!!" I couldn't, so I pushed myself as much as I could, fell, pulled my feet up close to me, and crawled as fast as I could away from it. Paul ran the snake away by beating on the bushes, then calmly told me to come on. I screamed, "NO! Come for me!" He said, "No way, just come on, or I'll leave you!" I was so scared, with no way to see the ground. I worked my way though, one step at a time, and then listened. We both also knew that where there was one snake, there was another mate close by. I made it unharmed with the thought at first with Paul's warning, he did care about me, but when he wouldn't come for me, he could care less. We didn't know at the time it would be our last run on the quad runner. The next time, we found out they had outlawed 4-wheelers from the forest. It was a big disappointment for us. Days before we went to ride, we had just bought a second one. Later, we were informed of designated areas designed for riders. No more riding in the forest. We tried the designated area it was just too dangerous.

Late one night, while we were camping, something woke me up, splashing and crashing. I went to the back of the camper to wake Paul and told him to listen. He said it sounded like Big-foot coming up the creek. A site of this creature had been reported years before. We went out to see, and it was the forestry workers breaking down the small dams that had been built by visitors over the season. The next morning, up early making coffee, I kept seeing things moving in the water. I was too far away to tell what they were, so I got my coffee and walked down to the creek. OH NO! I looked around my feet and couldn't see anything moving. I stood still just in case I missed any of them. Right before me were 22 water moccasins! In the water you could see them fine, but on the ground you could not see them. I dropped my cup and whistled for Paul. He started for me and I told him to look at the ground, and look hard. He said, "What is that moving around? Water moccasins!" He said some leaves were moving beside my foot and not to move. I have no idea how long I stood still, while he watched the snakes go back into the water. We knew that the forestry workers had broken up the snake's nest when they broke the dams, but we had never seen so many crawling on land before. I stayed close to camp until the next night. Paul went to take his bath, a few minutes later he came running back to camp for the flashlights. He said, "Come on, I have soap on me." I couldn't figure out what he wanted or what was going on. He wanted me to hold both of the big lights while he finished bathing. He told me not to get in the water, and about that time he said, "There, shine the beam over there!" There's no way I would have been in that water. Water moccasins coming from three sides with their pink mouths wide open, shining in the light. He splashed the water, but it didn't stop them. He wanted me to toss him a light; he saw he couldn't outrun them. He pounded them with the light and then he ran out. The next morning there were two of them dead up against a big rock. Other campers were coming in, and we warned them to stay out of the water. Our daughters spent 21 yrs in that creek and our grandchildren had played in it and had never been bitten.

There were not too many snake encounters after that. When I moved to another state, I had moved up close to an Indian reservation, where the buffalo roam. All behind my studio apartment were thick woods. There was no way you could you even think of going in there. One day I was very tired from working, and had stopped to get groceries on the way home. Once there, you had to park and then walk up a hill to a huge patio. I had both hands full of bags, and stepped up on the concrete. While I was walking to the stairs, something caught my eye. Well, maybe the neighbors had left something out. Then it moved. Lying two feet from me was a very long, thick snake. Standing there so tired, I looked at it; of course his head was up looking at me. I told him: "Now listen to me, you live in the woods and I live here. But one of us has got to go, and I'm too tired to go around." He never made a move toward me, just gave a flicker of his tongue. Neither of us was moving. I asked, "Well, what have you decided?" He turned his head the way he had been going in the first place and just crawled right off of the patio. Not long after, there were two more snakes crawling around the edge, not really bothering anyone.

This story isn't about a snake, but I didn't want to leave it out, because it happened at the same place as the last story.

A friend of mine, Milo, had come to visit from Europe. A few nights later, I was in the shower something caught my eye. So I screamed out, "HELP!" Milo came running to see what was wrong. I held the curtain out so he could see it and can you help me? He stood there shaking his hand, ready to jump up and down, asking, "What am I supposed to do with it?" I said, "Get it!" He was bouncing around and screaming, "With what, with what?" I stood there looking at him, and said, "Well, I thought I had a man in the house. Are you a man or mouse Milo?" He continued his charade saying, "Right now, A MOUSE!" Shaking my head I told him to get me a mayonnaise jar from the kitchen. I took the jar and thought it sure was hard to be a scared female when the man was more scared of the scorpion than you were. It was funny until a few days later, Another scorpion was in the kitchen sink and crawled on my hand. As I watched it, be it scorpion or a snake, I knew they wouldn't hurt you unless they felt fear or pain. I feel as if I'm living proof of it after I sent the scorpion back to the woods.

There's one more short story from the same area. An old restaurant had some of the best big burgers that you could ever put in your mouth. One burger would feed four people. As I left the restaurant, I went around the reservation hoping to see some wild animals. A small truck was up ahead blowing its horn. Looking around and taking my time, I kept wondering why were they blowing their horn. I couldn't see a thing. They flew on down the road. Just as I rounded the bend, glory be!!!!!! **Buffalo** were everywhere! Let me tell you they were HUGE!!!!!!!! I tried to just creep along, but when those big things get in front of you and behind you, leaving you no place to go, all you can do is come to a dead stop. Only once in my life had a buffalo charged me, and there I was in the middle of more than a hundred of them. No car was in sight, so I just sat there quietly. That must be the big papa and the others had to be the big mammas with babies. Anyone knows you should never look a wild animal in the eyes, especially one this big. Without a doubt I knew these big wild beasts could make mincemeat out of my car and me at any given time. It was so strange how they walked all around my car, sniffing; the babies didn't, they stayed back. A big one walked so close to the window it's hair left streaks on the glass. It took about thirty minutes for them to let me go. I guess they were satisfied after checking me out. A thought came to me, I sure was glad I ate a hamburger and not a **BUFFALO BURGER!**

Struggling . . .

You begin struggling when you first enter this world to take your first breath of air. Each day, you struggle to make accomplishments to get compliments. As the days, months, and years roll by, you continue to struggle to grow, learn, and survive. We seem to think once we finally reach adulthood that the struggling is over. Is that why we struggle so hard to get there? Or do we think we can stop struggling once we are grown and on our own? It's only the beginning!

There is something that the universe of parents has been struggling to accomplish; that is, to make their children grow up too fast. Teach them with their acknowledgement of life. With the exception of a few parents, most teach the basics of life: walk, talk, eat, watch television, play games and go to school. How many of us teach our children what it cost to maintain a life as an adult? Most children begin school with excitement, but after a year or two, they don't want to go. Why? That's easy. From the first day of life, we learn that there are *have to's* in our lives, with no choice in the matter in which we are situated. In our lives we cross more things we *have to do*, which override the *want to do*. When a child is in these situations with just *have to do,* it makes sense why so many children steal, break laws, do drugs and kill each other.

Do young adults really understand what they are doing when they make a child? By all means, I can say, I *did not* know what I was doing! So I know without a doubt that I passed my stupidity down to my children, and they will pass it to their own. It will continue until someone sees that it has to be changed. They must have knowledge and willpower to see that it is done. Parents don't spend much time with their children as a family, and if they do, it's because they *have to*, not *want to!* It's the same for the children. I don't care if you disagree or not, it is so true. Think about it when your family gathers. Be honest: if not to me, then to yourself.

How many older parents look back and say, "I wish I had it to do over again! It would be different! My life and my children's would have been so much easier." I'm guilty as sin, and can't even remember how many times I have said the same thing. But our mistakes are made, and we know for certain we cannot go back. Do you know why we say these words? Because we are finally grown! We can see our mistakes, and it would be so much easier to conduct ourselves in a more constructive way. We have knowledge of what life is really about. It's not our parents' faults anymore than it is ours. They were taught the same as we were, and it will continue . . . .

Think about this really hard. If our parents had had the knowledge to teach us in the beginning to look at life with a different positive outlook, would we have struggled so hard? Would our children? Our grandchildren? If we had the chance to do it over again, what would we change? What? Could we change our children's future? Could we make a difference in the world? It's not too late! We have children with children. We could start now. You say how? Ok, let's look at what we were taught. Or should it be what we were not taught? Life should be taught as an adventure with responsibilities. Adventures will take you to places of the unknown, and discoveries can be made every day, with the willpower to adventure one more step further in life. You can't wait for things to come to you, because you'll be waiting until death comes. You must reach into all things: words, books, documentaries, art, and so on. Never be afraid to ask a question, even though you may not get answers to them all. But there are answers, even if humans don't accept that they have sat back and never learned how to search, or research, for an answer. With computer knowledge in the space age of today, anything is possible. Always use your first instinct without fear or doubt. It's your sixth sense kicking in. Most people don't even know they have it, and don't try to use it. Many are afraid of the unexplained, and prefer to back away instead of facing it full charge. It's an adventure that carries us further into the unknown. We must explore with every option that is before us. Open the door and go. Challenge it, take your time to see and learn all. When you are young, there is no reason to "hurry up and be an adult!" Once you do grow up, the child in you must leave, so you can take on your responsibilities. This is another thing we should be taught as a child, the cost of being an adult. Take your time to grow up; with as many things as there are to learn on this earth, there is no reason to be bored, depressed, stressed, or even suicidal.

Find out what famous people did, and the way they lived. You may find your way to create something to help others who are afraid of a change in their lives. Sooner or later we all need help one way or another.

There are still things to be created and discovered in your life. Be strong, pack the bad things in life away, and keep walking. Maybe one day you can discover a way to prevent them from happening to someone else. Everything you learn will help you to succeed in a good, healthy life. You'll always need knowledge of the past to help you survive the future. As time goes by, the change is going to be harder than it was for the generations gone by.

Education is one of the greatest values in life, but there is one thing you should never forget, your common sense, because you will need it all of your life.

Conclusion

Ms. Kommenus sits alone with her thoughts of what the end should be; or should this be the end? One can only wonder. Maybe this isn't the end, but only the beginning. There are many more stories for Ms. Kommenus to write about her character Marion, as she sits there in a quiet little village of peace and serenity in Europe. She takes notice that the neighbors stay to themselves, only living the way they have been taught. They have no concern about anything she does, so she continues to create more stories.

The past several years have made her see why God allowed her to be there, why the world seems closed off from her. It was to write this book, in hopes of helping people who are abused, to give them hope for a better life. It was also to show them that no matter how bad things are, or if they feel as if no one loves them, even if depression deepens their minds with thoughts of suicide, there is always help. Maybe they can see there is always someone who loves them very deeply, and that is God! You can talk to God all you want, but you must be very sincere with Him; just let go, and He will help you by opening a door.

There is no way Ms. Kommenus's character Marion could have survived if she had not had faith. It led her to believe she could survive, and that it would get better. God had a plan for her. All of her help to others paid off, by making her as good as she could be. She always did what she thought was right from her heart, since she believes that is where Christianity began. She now sees what her sole purpose of staying alive all this time is for. So, this isn't the end for the character Marion, it's only the beginning. Ms. Kommenus closes now to leave you with her own poem of love:

LOVE

What is love?
Can you define love?
Where can you find love?

It is not here.
It is not there.
But, comes from where?

Love comes from the heart.
Love comes from the soul.
Love comes from within.

You must love yourself for it to be here.
You must love others for it to be there.

Then you will know where.

The Author

This is the first book by the author Acquanetta Kommenus. She was born in the southern states of America where, in her early years, she witnessed much abuse amongst her family, friends, classmates and co-workers. Living near to a chemical plant, she feels that this could have contributed to the many suicides, physical illnesses and abuse situations of which she writes. The stories and people of whom she relates are all fictional but are as real as life itself for those who have had the misfortune of experiencing any type of abuse in their own lives. Acquanetta has been encouraged by her friends around the world to write this book in the hope that it will give a deeper insight into the world of the abuser and the abused.

Having lived abroad for some years, Acquanetta has returned to her homeland where she has since married her very special man whose wonderful support and encouragement has made this book possible.

Made in the USA
Columbia, SC
07 May 2022